THE Steel Deal

JAMES BLAKLEY

THE POWERS THAT BE
PUBLISHING

Publisher: The Powers That Be Publishing

Paperback ISBN 978-1-7362537-0-0
eBook ISBN 978-1-7362537-1-7

1 3 5 7 9 10 8 6 4 2

Dedication

Thanks to God for everything. First, for giving me a wonderful, hard-working family, who raised me, supported me when I was nothing, and encouraged me to achieve my first feat of fiction. For the blessing of tremendously talented teachers, professors, friends, and colleagues who helped broaden my mind. For the flair for fiction and for the guts to go where I've had to in order to make it grow. And finally, for three great states among the fabulous fifty: Missouri (where I learned what I know); Kansas (where I've used it to survive); and Oregon (where Inkwater Press's top-notch editing, production design, and customer service assistance to The Powers That Be Publishing has given me the opportunity to thrive).

Contents

Prologue

I got home after six in the morning without a hitch. The elevator ride up to my apartment was the only nerve-racking thing. The creaking and groaning of the pulleys always made me feel like being in a coffin: that I was being buried when going down, exhumed when coming up. And when I felt great – which wasn't very often – I was awakened to the reality that one snap of the worn wires could really send me diving several floors to a crushing death.

It would be good exercise to take the stairs. But I wouldn't make the seven flights to my apartment... alive. I was getting old. At 55, conservation of time, money, and energy are top priorities. That's why I risked what life I had on the elevator.

Ironically, the rest of my aged, art deco–styled apartment complex had been recently renovated courtesy of the local historical society. The exterior was repainted, the interior supplied with potted ferns (that are tall and better taken care of than the tenants), and newfangled LCD lights decorated the main lobby. But beyond the entryways, they didn't do squat. It's like a facelift: your mug may look magnificent, but typically you can't afford the other nips and tucks. In the end, the rest of you still looks like a raisin.

So the elevator still whined and occasionally lurched. But I survived the ride up and the walk down the dimly lit hall to my apartment. I got inside and locked the door. Exhausted, I wrenched myself out of my windbreaker and hauled off my holster, which was saddled down with my gun, flashlight, and walkie-talkie.

Next, I went for the light switch. But someone was polite enough to flip it for me.

"Thanks," I told the guest behind me. Another guest sat motionless on my couch.

I felt the guest who'd flipped the lights on now at my feet. I looked down and saw him take my revolver from the holster on the floor. Within seconds, he pressed the revolver against my back and moved me toward the couch. We stopped, and the guest with my gun walked around into view. His body – beefy, broad-shouldered, and covered in a red, all-leather letterman jacket – barely contained its hoodlum's hostility. And below the slightly turned sideways brim of a Cincinnati Reds ball cap, the young man's yellowish-brown face – sprouting a goatee – spit unfriendliness at me.

Ziggy Steed, the guest who got the lights and my gun, didn't take a seat on the couch because his job was to intimidate me with muscle-and-muzzle. That is better done when standing – posturing. It was the guy on the couch whose job it was to intimidate me mentally. That is better done sitting (like you're behind a corporate or government desk).

Ziggy's seated overseer was a thin man, but not skinny. He was lead pipe lean. And skin the color of coal was smeared over that pipeline physique. One velvety-looking trouser leg was crossed over the other and sparkle-rimmed spectacles encased a stare that was vacant but suddenly occupied me. It all gave him a rather elegant look that didn't fit my low-end setting. Except that his business was a down and dirty one: collection. So he was right at home.

The man on my couch unfolded his hands – whose fresh manicure shined like snow against his dark skin – from their formerly patient position on his lap. When he spoke, it was in English, but with a noticeable accent. He sounded like '80s Kansas City Chiefs running back Christian Okoye, "The Nigerian Nightmare." "You're not spooked at our wake-up call?" Solomon "Sully" Styles asked.

"How do you spook *a spook*?" I asked.

"What?" The old racial slur sailed over Sully's bald head.

"Anyway, my phone's disconnected. So, I figured you'd contact me somehow."

"Makes sense," Sully said.

"Yeah, but what I need are dollars."

"Two thousand of them, to be exact," Sully reminded me. "Mister Grimes wants to know your progress – how close you are to settling up."

"I remember I had a grand left, and two weeks to pay it."

"You were late with an installment," Sully answered.

"Two grand," I repeated the inflated figure. Then I did some quick loan shark arithmetic aloud. "A missed payment, plus the interest, and you guys' fees: it figures."

"You're too chilly," Sully carped. "You take the fun out of the collection biz."

"You mean by not crying and begging for mercy? I knew what I was getting into. Besides, at my age, I can't afford to get too excited. Gator might get a corpse, not cash."

"A corpse's organs are valuable," Sully said. Then he flashed a sadistic smile. "And so are a *live* body's. You can live with one lung, one kidney."

"Do you *really* want my organs, Sully? They're smoked and soaked in over a quarter century of spirits!"

Sully chuckled. "You're just too chilly," he

repeated. "That's why Mister Grimes digs you I guess." Then Sully got serious. "Mister Grimes says he'll settle for the original grand...but *by Saturday*. You'll have one more week to pay off the rest."

"How about some refreshments, fellas? You know, bread or water?" I offered.

Sully declined. "We gotta fly," he said.

"But don't you fly...*outta town*," Ziggy growled. He finally got into the act. I wondered if they practiced that, if there was a Collection Threat Choreography class they attended. *Nah.* With so many collection calls, when could Ziggy and Sully study?

Sully grinned and left through the front door that I graciously held open for him.

Ziggy flung my .357 on the floor and headed for the door, too. He chose not to be as graceful in his exit as Sully. Ziggy's leather-covered largeness nearly squished me against the doorframe. It was a reminder: my guests meant business.

Both disappeared down the hall and into the elevator. I hoped it would crash. But Gator would only send more collectors my way. And they wouldn't be as professional as my departed guests. When they were gone, I shut the door and collapsed. And it wasn't just from working eight hours on the job.

CHAPTER ONE

Catch Up

When I awoke, it was about 10 AM. I went to the window. Outside was cloudy; the sun again powerless to puncture the steel-gray gloom beyond. It looked like rain, but probably wouldn't. A trick the atmosphere plays on the city, the weather people say. I was used to it; just another dingy daybreak. The sun eventually breaks through, typically around noon. Luckily, the weird weather pattern lasts from late spring into early summer.

I wished the clouds that hung over my life were just a passing event. Instead, they were part of a gloom that lasts longer than the seasonal morning variety. It was smog. And like smog, the big-city demands were choking the life out of me, making it hard to see how I would make it through each day with a roof still over my head.

It was getting to everyone it seemed. Pessimism was a tradition, rather than a passing fad. It seemed there used to be a breather between wars and depressions, where people could hope, create, and prosper. Not anymore.

The relentless rise of greed and corruption reached a point where the public perception almost permanently dimmed. People's skepticism was such that they didn't quickly seek the services of private sleuths anymore. Guys like me: whose job it is to help the cops keep an even keel. But people think, what good could a single sleuth be against so much sleaze? They even suspect detective agencies of being crooked. In an agency, they think you're part of the system: bound by the brass and reduced by red tape.

So business slowed to catsup speed and that left me in the red – deep in debt, I mean. And for awhile, that's all I could do was play catch up: catch up with my bills, anyway. As for catching up with the times, forget it. My car was a crusty clunker, whose repairs kept me from having the dough for a cell phone or a personal computer.

And my detecting skills steadily diminished. Instead of staking out suspects, I staked out the tracks for tips on the ponies. And the only clues I looked for were what lucky number combinations worked best for picking winning lottery numbers.

I told myself gambling was like buying stock:

you research the company, buy-in, and watch the daily ticker to see if you got ahead. But I rarely did.

Yesterday's horse, Second Wind, never got his. So I didn't get mine. Lagging at the clubhouse turn, he finished fourth. And my lottery numbers also failed to win, place, or show. That's how Gator Grimes entered the picture.

Grimes and I are about the same age. He's better looking and lives large, if only from loan sharking's steep interest. But if the Bible's right, that "the love of money is the root of all evil," at least my poor soul is in better shape to enter the pearly gates than Grimes's greedy one.

It's hard to believe we share some of the same life experiences, mainly braving the barely integrated '60s and early '70s. Grimes had it tougher, coming from down South; me, a bit easier, coming from the Midwest. I'm convinced that's why he cut me some slack with the payoff. But to show a soft side would reduce his robber baron's rep to rubble.

I borrowed $500 from Grimes to cover the gambling losses, and it blew up into $1,500! I was able to keep pace by draining my savings. Then, I missed a payment somewhere and it ballooned to two grand. I still had $400 from my last payday; so I only needed $600 to cover the $1,000 I owed in four days. But I wanted rid of Grimes for good, and needed $1,600 to get off his hook.

The $400 starter came from my second job as a

night shift security guard. Seeing the tightening economic times, I hedged my bets a few years back and got my security guard's certification, even though I hate guard duty. Whether protecting people or property, there's little action in it. It's mostly standing around *looking* tough. And at my age, just trying to look alive each day is a challenge!

On the bright side of my night job, the pay was steady – an instant advantage over being a private eye. Guarding stores and driving night deposits to the bank also kept my observation skills sharp. Being able to size up a situation is a key part of doing well as a detective.

And since I had to pawn my piece, the security guard gig gave me a gun. For the most part, a gun isn't necessary for being a good detective. But it's handy to have ready because smog isn't the only dirty element in this city (as Grimes's guys proved).

Dirty element got me thinking about my clunker Oldsmobile. Usually, my four-wheeled fossil farted extra exhaust and groaned from faulty suspension. It was nothing serious or damaging, other than to my pride (which was shot to hell anyway). But when I hopped in and started out to scare up some scratch by Saturday, my Oldsmobile lurched and rattled. And for what little money I had, I bet it on the transmission going bad. *Damn!*

Then again, I was no expert with cars. I wish I was. I could have a skill that is in constant demand.

Maybe my notions about what was the matter with the Olds were wrong or exaggerated. Once when it died on me, I thought I'd have to spend a fortune on another car. Fortunately, it turned out that the battery connectors were bad. But it still cost $150 to find that out and to get it fixed. I hoped it was something similarly mild this time.

I slipped on a black short-sleeved polo shirt. That way, if the diagnosis for the Olds turned out to be terminal, I'd be dressed for mourning. I hauled myself into a pair of blue jeans and pulled on my best pair of jogging shoes (in case the Olds died en route). All saddled up, I locked the apartment door and headed out again.

CHAPTER TWO

To Cruise Again

My apartment complex's parking lot is big, but it wasn't hard finding my Olds. It was the rusty, tan-colored relic: the thorn among the other rosier-looking and rosier-running rides. I found it, unlocked the door, and climbed in.

Settling into the cracked leather interior and inspecting the dusty gauges made me as anxious as one of those Apollo astronauts must have been before lifting off for the moon. And whenever driving the Olds, I told myself I was merely an explorer, too – but more like Columbus, in one of his creaky sailing ships, than an astronaut.

A spaceman's got millions of bucks' worth of high-tech gadgets and geniuses on the ground to guide him. All Columbus and me had were the sun and moon. And still, old Chris had more than me because at times, the smog makes the sun hard to pinpoint.

Instead of worrying about what was wrong, I simply calculated the mission possibilities *should* it be that my transmission was to die. What if the car – I mean, ship – sank? How would the natives respond once I rowed ashore and entered their neighborhood? And would the re-supply ship – tow truck – arrive in time to rescue me?

Well, the most important leg of the journey got off without delay: the car started. My nerves eased, and I steered the Olds out of the lot, down the street, and into the busy intersection. I drove like the old days (when the speed limit was 55). Even though I stayed in the slowest of the three lanes – closest to the shoulder, so I could pull off if I stopped – I still got a lot of disapproving honks from faster drivers. But at least I wouldn't blow a gasket or overheat the engine by driving fast, and stall.

My painstaking planning and plodding pace paid off when, about a half hour later, I arrived safely at my destination, Cruise Again Auto Repair (or CAR for short). I parked and happily planted my feet (instead of another flag of discontent) on the ground.

Cruise Again is a two-story affair, with its clean, blue-tiled floor lobby occupying the top floor and its five large bays below. I headed for the lobby when suddenly a voice shouted to me. I turned around and looked down. A familiar smiling face came out from the third bay below. And its greasy hand waved for me to come on down. It was Hubert "Hub" Wheeler.

Like many mechanics, the daily doses of dirt, grease, and grime make Hub look older than he is. He's only thirty-something years old, but is the heart and soul of Cruise Again. He owns the place! He's also the head mechanic – the messiah who regularly resurrects my ride from rust in peace to rejuvenate; from rust to rust, back to reliable.

As with many masterminds, though, Hub has a quirky side. It's not his beat-up John Deere ball cap (whose green color clashes with his blue jumpsuit) or the beer belly that belies his brilliance. It's his mouth: it's faster than a fan belt and a one-track rant about how the system's forever sticking it to us. When I tow my chronically ill Olds into Cruise Again, I get a lecture that I make sure Hub doesn't include in the labor charge.

"Yeah, Sonny," Hub began, "if those Motor City fat cats could make cars out of stainless steel, we wouldn't have to buy one so often. And did you know they got vehicles – not test ones you see all shined up at them auto shows, but ones ready to roll – that get damned near a hundred miles to the gallon?"

"Yep," I replied.

There was a *thud!* It was the sound of Hub's head

hitting the hood. He appeared from his work below in wide-eyed surprise. "You've really seen one!" Hub sputtered.

"Even rode one once." I could no longer conceal a rascally grin and replied, "They're called mopeds, Hub."

"Not *scooters*, Sonny! I'm talking about real cars!" Hub dismissed my revelation and returned to work. "Hell, forget about cars and bikes for a minute and think about what runs them: energy. Think about them running on the energy between mass instead of mass itself."

"Now you've really lost me," I admitted.

"Free energy, Sonny: no oil, no solar, no electricity! That's why they don't make them though."

"Who doesn't make them?"

"The oil companies: That's who. If they made free energy cars, they'd be dancin' with the train."

"Dancing with a…"

"Committing suicide – financially, I mean. They'd be puttin' themselves out of business. But they can't hold back alternative energy forever, Sonny. The word will get out sooner or later, and there will be another big revolution! If you want to make some money, Sonny, look into that alternative energy thing sometime."

Hub eventually gets his weird thought process moving as usefully as the gears and levers in the clunkers he fixes. Finally, Hub came to a conclusion about my car.

"It's the carburetor," he told me. "The fuel mix is too lean."

"What do you mean?"

"I mean a carburetor controls the fuel and air mix. Fuel injectors do that nowadays, but you got an older car. You probably just got a bunch of dirt clogging the jets or jamming up the bowl."

I sighed, "So what's the damage, *to my wallet*, I mean?"

"Just the price of a bottle of carburetor cleaner, probably," Hub replied. "If not, just some new spark plugs. I'll take her for a spin; then, I'll know for sure.

"Having a gimpy carburetor's not all bad I guess. It's kind of like smoking: you're killing your lungs with all that gunk, but slowly. You don't really realize the damage until one day, you can't run or do anything fast anymore without a lung transplant. Can they transplant lungs, Sonny?"

"If they can, we'll all be standing in line – a long line – for new ones," I sighed, referring to our daily intake of smog.

"You really need a newer car, Sonny."

"Look, Hub, all I want from my car is for it to get me from one end of town to the other. It doesn't have to look 25 or drive 65, so long as *I* arrive."

"Yeah, but you wanna get there in time and maybe in a little style, don't ya? I mean maybe that's why you're out of work so much lately, Sonny. Maybe…"

Suddenly, somebody shouted "Sonny" again. Though loud, the voice was a relief from Hub's. It belonged to Meiko McCall, Cruise Again's receptionist extraordinaire.

"Speaking of jobs, maybe Meiko's got one for me," I told Hub as I left the floor.

"In your dreams, Sonny!" Hub hollered.

"Wipe all that grime on something besides your mind!" I hollered back.

But my mind was as dirty as Hub's. Because of all the bodies at Cruise Again, Meiko McCall's is the least in need of repair. Her young, oval face doesn't require mounds of makeup to magnetize men. It's bracketed by straightened hair that is long and as shiny-black as a country night. Today, it was pinned up in a pony tail. But she let the bangs tickle her eyes: eyes that are easy to read and colored chestnut brown, like her skin.

Meiko wore a classy blue denim shirt with the sleeves rolled and the collar flipped. A fashionable ostrich skin belt spanned her slim waist. Matching blue denim jean Capri pants housed her curvaceous caboose. And all of that was balanced on a shapely set of wheels that, in my dreams, danced and dealed for dollars when off duty.

At first glance, the whole outfit resembled the mechanics' navy blue jumpsuits (minus the strappy, yellow stack heels and matching bird skin belt, of course). As if Meiko would get in there and actually get down and dirty with repair work, if she had to.

But what little chivalry Hub's techs and mechanics had wouldn't allow Meiko to break a nail on anything but the calculator. Hub wasn't stupid enough to allow part of Cruise Again's appeal to tarnish from the oil and grime from the toil of the bays below.

But Meiko was on the road to places bigger than CAR. A modeling agency, maybe? Not unless she ran it because Meiko has what my generation calls *spunk*. It's a high-octane blend of style, smarts, and motivation that doesn't seem to drive today's workforce: an age group that as a rule doesn't see the value in taking personal pride in their jobs.

But when I cleared the final step to the lobby, Meiko's chic, corporate cool finally cracked. "Take the damn phone, Sonny!" she demanded. I took the cordless receiver, but had to take my punishment too: Meiko's solid left fist dug hard into my arm. "Since when did I become *your* secretary?" she wanted to know.

"Since my phone got disconnected," I boldly replied. "Hub said I can forward my calls here. It's just for a few days, until I can get the phone turned on and buy an answering machine."

"Why don't you just get with the program and buy a cell phone?" Meiko asked.

I grinned and remarked, "Funny how you never suggest that I just buy a new car."

"I'm not stupid!" the receptionist replied, stomping back into the lobby with me gladly in her sweet-scented tow. "The business your twenty-year-old wreck rolls in is…"

"*Twenty-six years,*" I interrupted Meiko. *And definitely older than you*, I thought.

Meiko plopped down at her desk. "We were talking about cell phones," she said.

"And why I don't have one," I added. "As to the "why," haven't you seen the average cell bill? About $800 a year, they say, minus the options. And with all the twisted terms, you have to hire a lawyer to translate the contract and a banker to help finance a second mortgage to pay the damned thing.

"Besides, don't you know how may wrecks are caused by people yapping on those things while driving?"

"No," was Meiko's uninterested reply, as she pored over her piles of paperwork.

"*What?* Hub didn't tell you?"

The receptionist's brown eyes rolled. "Spare me, Sonny!"

"*Anytime*," I coolly offered to rescue the receptionist. "Just give me a ring. I've always wanted a secretary."

Through a smirk, Meiko grunted, "You couldn't afford me, Sonny."

Yeah, Meiko was going places…but sadly, it would be without me in tow. Her Ferrari of a façade was just too quick for my wit that was always stuck in reverse and for my wallet that was regularly running on empty.

So finally, I took the call. The voice on the other end was feminine. But was it beautiful? "Mister Busco?" it asked.

"Sonny Busco here," I said.

"Mister Busco, I need your help!" the voice pleaded.

Oh, yeah! What my ears heard was eye-catching all right. But when you live in a city full of smog, you wonder sometimes whether what you're sensing is real.

I'd got wind of something big. But was it bouquet or bullshit I smelled in the distressed damsel's $2,500 offer?

Back in the Black

I *need help. Help me. Can you help me? Spare me.* They're choruses so commonly heard in my line of work that I could put them to music and maybe make some real money. That is if I had some musical talent beyond that of a critic. But that desperate-sounding phone call was the sweetest sound I'd heard in months. Like the Fairy Godmother calling Cinderella. And it seemed I too was dancing again, to the beat of Pink Floyd's hit "Money." I could dig myself out of the debt I owed Gator Grimes and have a little left over. Not enough left to "buy a new car or caviar," as one line from "Money" suggests, but enough to at least finally pay off a payday loan that nagged at me.

I told Hub Wheeler I had a job. And I told him what he always wanted to hear: that the job was exciting, risky, and involved saving the world. Honestly though, I only knew it promised to pay well (which in my condition was all I really cared about).

But Hub was so excited about my prospects that he insisted I drive a different car. He even promised to fix the Olds for a percentage of whatever my exciting, world-saving undertaking raked in. The offer cost me nothing but a little sincerity, so I bought in.

I followed Hub around the back of Cruise Again to his rental/used car lot. There were about twenty or so cars corralled in the high, chain-link fenced lot. There were no trucks. Just sedans and one convertible coupe: none of them special. Most were middle- to high-mileage models with the domed, aerodynamic design of the '90s. The rest had the long-bodied, luxury look of the '80s. The convertible was grayish, but the sedan paintjobs ranged from red to dark blue.

All would have been perfect rides for detective work because they were ordinary. They didn't draw attention. Instead, we passed them and arrived at Hub's idea of an appropriate auto.

"Here's what you want, Sonny," Hub told me. "It's the poor man's Camaro." I winced at the reminder of my economic status (for which Hub apologized). Hub then swept his arm over the hood with a car show model's grace, as if to unveil it to the world. Then he proudly announced, "May I introduce you to the Dodge Stealth."

I gave the car the once-over, walking around it and looking inside. "Nice," I replied mildly. *Nice... for impressing a high school date,* was what I really thought.

Though it was an older model, the car should have been called Standout, instead of Stealth. The sports car's structure was slick and sporty, with a stylish spoiler that screamed for attention. But it did have one thing going for it: it had a jet black paint job.

I was reminded of that old racial rallying cry from my youth. *Black is beautiful.* I laughed to myself and looked for something positive in the sports car. If this was that radar-deflecting bomber kind of black, the Stealth would be perfect for slipping police speed traps. And black lends itself well to late-night stakeouts. Maybe Hub had a point when he picked the Stealth for me to drive. So I thanked him, hopped in, and headed out.

I was in the black again – if only it meant being in a black car. So, I needed to look capable for a woman willing to pay me more than I had lately made in a month. I stopped at home to change clothes before meeting my client.

I'm old school: so a tie and jacket were in order. After a cold shower to whet the senses and a dash of cologne and pats of talcum powder, I slipped into an extra large fit, medium blue Oxford shirt. It could easily look casual, if I lost the crimson-colored power tie with a microdot design that I chose to wear with it. I pulled on a pair of navy blue trousers; laced up some sensible, rubber-soled dress shoes (that I shined up with petroleum jelly); and donned a blue blazer that wasn't quite the same shade of blue as the trousers. I looked myself over in the medicine cabinet mirror of my shoebox-sized bathroom. I came across as at least middle-class competent.

Once dressed, I went down the hall and asked a neighbor if I could use his phone. When I told him it was an emergency, he said "no sweat, my man" and let me in. I rang Coast is Clear Security. The only thing I liked about them, besides being paid regularly, was their motto: "Whenever We're Near, the Coast is Clear." I gave them a straightforward story that I was sick and couldn't report for duty. They probably didn't buy it, but maybe I got points for not saying something obviously fake like I was dying or someone I knew was dying. Or that I was dying to know someone who was dying because they might leave me an inheritance.

Giving Coast a ring reminded me I'd forgotten something. When I got back to my apartment, I went into the bedroom again. I removed my blue blazer and slung my shoulder holster. Then I removed a double-action Magnum .357 revolver from its lockbox.

While the company gun skimped on capacity (holding only five rounds), it sure looked good – with black rubber grips that nixed some of the nasty recoil and a brushed metal finish that made the piece look platinum. I'd have made for one slick stiff when the coroner "pried it from my cold, dead hand", as the saying goes. A hand attached to a body blasted by a criminal's bigger bullet ability.

Coast issued the gun because of its newfangled alloy construction: it made it fairly lightweight for such a powerful caliber. As a result, it was easier to quick-draw and to carry – ideal for women and old men like me to handle.

The gun belonged in my uniform's belt holster. But it was small enough to fit in a pocket. I didn't like stashing a firearm in something as loose-fitting as pants or shirt pockets. So I managed to secure the revolver in my shoulder holster (which was actually designed for a .38).

Thankfully, the .357 easily fit beneath my blazer. The only bumpiness came from the shoulder holster's hard-shell. But it's easier to quick-draw from its sturdy pouch than from the softer stretch of a leather holster (which will sometimes tangle a gun).

I was finally set. So I locked up and headed for the Stealth. It felt strange knowing that I wouldn't have to think about *this* car breaking down. So what the hell would I have to think about? As it turned out, I had plenty.

I'd never got used to the low-riding feel of most sports cars. The Stealth's carriage was so near to the ground that I swore my pants felt the pavement, not the seat. Speaking of seats, the driver's side was obviously designed for people under six feet tall. I fit myself in, but sympathized with how crowded the bullets in my gun forever felt.

Next, I fretted over running the loaner car's air conditioner or turning on the stereo for fear of losing the edge my rattletrap Olds gave me. Rolling down all four of the Olds' windows (in order to feel the tease of a cool breeze) got me used to the near hundred degree heat that sizzles sometimes for weeks in late summer. The Olds' broken car antenna limited me to listening to mostly local AM oldies music. I didn't mind. In fact, those '60s and '70s singers were like old friends riding along, their songs bringing back memories of happier times that were full of possibility.

In a way, the Olds felt like a cocoon from the city's increasingly complex culture. Lately, though, I wished to come out of that old car with more than an appreciation of the past. I wanted to be recent, rich, and ready to fly the lower income coop.

Maybe that's why I was finally seduced by the Stealth. I thought, *you're not getting any younger: so enjoy it!* I found myself falling hard for the Stealth's revamped upholstery and how it incredibly gave off the new car scent: that near erotic automobile aroma that reels everybody in for a ride. The control panel's electronic twinkle, the smooth contoured seating, and the light hum beneath me when the sports car began to roll finally hooked me. I was cheating on my Olds. But it had cheated me out of countless dollars over the years. So, I soared carefree with the flow of freeway traffic as it snaked toward downtown.

From far-off, it looked like the city was ready to sink into saffron-colored sunset. But things changed on the last stretch of freeway in. What had looked like orange air darkened to an orangish-brown – the kind of brown that's found on rotten fruit. When I looked at my watch and realized evening was still a few hours off, I knew I'd been fooled. The sunset was smog.

This time, the sun was a familiar ball, but one whose strength was scattered through the gloom. It looked more like a headlight, and I could look at it without burning my eyes. The whole set-up gave the city a burnt, almost hellish, cast. And only the tallest of the lean, steel-boned, glass-skinned skyscrapers broke free. The smaller buildings were trapped and resembled tombstones rising.

After almost an hour of driving in the Stealth, the car began to feel like a casket. Its tinted windows made it hard to see out. The air that was once cool lost its bite and became lukewarm. It felt like the smog had seeped in and sapped my edge. All I could think about was that B.B. King blues ballad "The Thrill Is Gone."

Maybe it was just the reality that I was back in the badlands, that the time to battle whatever was to be my client's concern was closing in. I needed to regain my Olds edge. I needed a jolt.

CHAPTER FOUR

What a Wake-up

For most, a splash of water to the face is enough of a wake-up. But for me, I prefer a fistful of bourbon to the face. And while I could easily get liquor anywhere in town, nowhere served up a stiff slug to the senses like the Skyview Lounge.

The Lounge is a high-rise escape from the many fry-and-fly dives littering street level. I had some time to kill before meeting my client. So I turned off the freeway onto the boulevard. Ten minutes later, Heavenly High-Rise – home to the Lounge – was in sight. I drove into the lower level garage, parked, and took the elevator up.

When the door opened, the Lounge's clean, airy interior instantly breathed life back into me. The mood lighting was cupped in metal shades along the wall and released a just-right mix of orange and blue – the kind of blend you see in silver screen sunsets. The trendy leather-seated booths lining the walls were already full of couples. The main dining area was still mostly empty, but set. Some tables had more informal settings: clear red and blue plastic cups and yellow plates; others more intimate, with fancy vases full of fancy flowers, crystal stemware, sparkling silverware, and china rimmed with fake gold.

I waded through the gathering off-work crowd to the bar (which is a circular setup raised just above the dining area). I bellied up and ordered a double Old Grand-Dad on the rocks from the swarm of stacked high spirits. A junior barman (neatly dressed in a red jacket, crisp white shirt, and a bow tie) slid a tumbler of glistening ice cubes floating in a pool of copper-colored Kentucky bourbon down the countertop and into my hand. Now for the reason I loved the Lounge – the view.

To me, late afternoon is when this city is at its most stunning. That's usually about the time when rain – when it rains – lets up. It's also when the haze lifts and, when it's sunny, everything is drenched in golden afterglow. I strolled beyond the floor-to-ceiling glass windows along the west side of the Lounge and onto the balcony.

A descending mantle of heavy purple already began mashing the fizzling day deep into the horizon like a cigarette butt. A cool evening breeze blew in and rustled the patio plants' exotic leaves.

And with some '70s-style soul (sung by the modern-day Lisa Stansfield) surging through the sound system, I cursed myself for wasting what little cash I had on bourbon. My surroundings were intoxicating enough. *Damn, what a wake-up!*

Back inside, the Lounge smelled of Kansas City steak sizzling. But I didn't have the time or money for it. Suddenly someone bawled, *"Big Money, Sonny!"* It came from Joey the head barman, in what always sounded like authentic Brooklyn brio.

While he may not be from New York (or even directly from *the old country*) Joey is Italian for sure. He's got that bit of Mediterranean tan dusting his skin and tight, wavy dark hair. I suspect his accent is hyped Italian. Similarly some black hip-hop artists' hardcore slanging and banging is hyped for the cameras. When the limelight dies, so do their lies as most retire to the plush, patently suburban surroundings their acts afford them.

I'm not *that* cynical whenever I hear Joey. Besides adding more pizzazz to the Lounge, Joey's act breaks what must be the day-to-day dullness of dispensing drinks.

Joey was wearing a red dress shirt with the collar unbuttoned and black slacks. He shouldered the black bar towel he mopped the counter with and moseyed over to me. Leaning over the countertop, Joey reached out and fingered the lapel of my blazer.

"Buon gusto, bro," Joey remarked, making his

fingers into that typecast steeple and kissing them off from his lips.

"The 'bro' translated," I said, "but do I want to know what the rest means?"

A friendly smile creased Joey's jack-o-lantern-sized lid. "Yeah," he said. "It means you got class: you look sharp, Money."

"Thanks, Joey," I said, returning his friendly smile with one of my own.

"Forget about it," he said. Joey nestled his elbow on the counter and settled in for a bit. "So, you finally got a date or what?" he asked.

"Sort of," I replied.

Joey then asked, "Is it with a bookie, a bill collector, or broad?"

"All three," I answered. Then I ordered a Michelob Dark chaser.

"With all those people to see, you'll want to be quick on your feet, Money. So I'd better get you a *light* beer."

I threw up my hands in defeat. "You're the barman."

Joey came back, but he was empty-handed. He looked at me skeptically. "Money, I think you're going out with a broad," Joey concluded. "No one dresses sharp for a bookie or a bill collector! You want them to think you're broke, not in the money. But for a broad, you want her to think you're in the money, not broke. *Capisce?*"

I laughed at the logic and came clean. "Pick up the dice, you've won."

But for Joey DiFatino, that wasn't enough. He wanted the full scoop. "So, is she blond, brunette, or red-headed?" he hounded me. "Fake, flat, or…?"

"When I asked for a chaser, Joey, I expected beer, not trivial pursuit," I said. "You know, you'd make a good tabloid reporter – better yet, a member of the paparazzi!"

Joey gave me a snide grin before giving me my draft. "*Vaffanculo a Lei!*" he snarled. "And you *don't* wanna know what that one means."

"Well, at least you smiled when you said it. And none of those cuss words sounded like the 'N' word." I sipped the light beer – a champagne-colored brew called *Select 55*. Until inflation bogged it down, it was called "the lightest beer in the world." "Okay," I gave-in some to Joey's questioning, "the lady I'm seeing has a silver box."

Joey gawked. "You grave-robbing gigolo: you going with geezers now?"

I chuckled, "For a fat guy, you have the thinnest mind."

"Thin: like one of them laser pointers and always locked in," Joey said proudly.

"Well, re-tune that laser, Joey, because you're off the mark. I mean she has a silver box with her – like a case. Probably a purse," I tried to clarify my silver box slip-up.

"Silver, silver," Joey repeated to himself: "Is this lady a banker or something?"

"*It's just a color, Joey!* What are we playing, charades now?" I wanted to know.

Joey kept going. "Well, how old is she then?"

"Old enough," was all I would say.

"If you know how old she is, Money, she can't be a lady," Joey concluded.

"I don't get you."

"You know what they say about women and their ages: a lady never tells."

"And a gentleman never asks," I finished saying the old line. "But I'm a private dick, remember, Joey? It's my job to pry and poke into people's private parts."

It took a minute for Joey's memory to jog over his mounds of flesh. But when my attempt at crude humor finally hit, the shockwave from the bartender's hysterical howl bowled me into the elevator. *"You got a client?"* I heard Joey shout as the door shut.

The chauffeured ride to the garage was as cool going down as the last swig of beer. The upper crust perks of the Lounge were just what I needed. They made me feel like the best damned detective in the world; I'd regained my edge, my swagger.

I gazed out the glass-paneled elevator at the sweeping evening view of a re-charged city. Its arteries flowing with people racing to paint the town red. But that edge poked me, and I thought for a moment.

In a big city, red had many meanings. Would it be the scarlet sort that slithers from the shot, the stabbed – the slain? Or maybe it would just be cordial cherry or burgundy: as in a brand that's poured. Or was it some unknown kind of red?

Soon, there was a slight bump beneath my feet. I looked up to see the level indicator flash "G". It was the ground floor. It was back to the garage, and finally time to get it on.

CHAPTER FIVE

A Lady Tells

My watch said thirty minutes…thirty minutes until I met my client. But with early evening traffic moving like molasses, I was sweating it. I finally navigated Eventide Boulevard and peeled off the main drag. Twenty minutes had ticked away; ten were left.

I zoomed past the busy new strip mall on Tenth Street to the low-end lengths of Fifth. I swung the Stealth around the corner and whizzed toward a single-story liquor store and a single-story bar. There was a sliver of empty alley lodged between the two. That's where I stashed the Stealth.

I got out and hoofed it to the sidewalk with two minutes to spare. There I waited, fluttering like a bug between the attraction of brightly lit booze on display in the barred store window in front of me and on the neon bar sign above. All the while trying to stay on the lookout for – *that crazy kid!*

There were several screeches, honks, and angry hollers from drivers who narrowly missed hitting a careless pedestrian – a girl. Nothing for me to care about... that is until I saw what the girl carried. A glittering case: a silvery box. The girl zigzagged her way toward my side of Fifth. Alcohol's appeal suddenly diminished. Instead, my eyes fixed on the increasing intensity of the case, and I moved toward its carrier. I stopped halfway and gave the girl a wave. She saw me and carefully walked up.

We met at last, but the girl said nothing. What words didn't communicate, her eyes easily did. They were wide and full of fear, the pinpoint pupils racing like heart monitor blips that measured me for authenticity. I finally flashed a friendly smile and told her, "Nice box."

The girl looked at the case in hand and told me thanks. *"Oh!"* she said as if suddenly remembering something else. "I thought..." The girl stalled. She became lost in thought. Then it came to her. "I thought girls with glasses never get passes," she blurted.

"With a box like yours," I coolly replied, "I'm surprised you don't get more."

This time, the girl was on cue. "Do you want to see more, Mr. Busco?" she asked.

I smiled and answered, "Absolutely, Ms. Sage."

With our identities confirmed, the girl and I split for the Stealth. We hopped in. I flipped the lights, rolled the tinted power windows, and revved the engine. I geared up and we sped toward uptown's torrent of traffic.

While my new client's driver's license said she was 27, at first she seemed more like a prim, teen-aged honor student. Pixy Sage was a petite jumble of nerves. She had this Catholic schoolgirl get-up going, with a modest black skirt and white blouse covering her thin frame. A short, platinum blonde-ish do that was tousled on top plastered Pixy's large head. And black, square-framed glasses teetered on a small, straight nose.

One thing seemed to redeem my client, though: her leather boots. Go-go styled and nearly knee-high, they shined black like the asphalt they pounded and betrayed a bold streak.

"Sorry I ruined the secret phrase we agreed on, Mr. Busco," Pixy apologized. "Looks like I'm a bad actor."

"Well, at least you're honest about it. Honesty is as rare in this town as fresh air is to breathe," I told her. "Now, you told me over the phone to pick up you and a silver box on Fifth – done. And you mentioned paying me twenty-five hundred dollars, to do what?"

"Is that not enough?" Pixy asked nervously.

"Maybe or maybe not," I replied. "Depends

on what you want done. If it involves drugs or hot property…"

"Oh, no, Mr. Busco: it's nothing like that!" Pixy replied.

I pounded my hand on the steering wheel. *"Damn!"* I complained.

Pixy gasped, "You mean you'd actually transport drugs or stolen property, if the price was higher? Maybe you're not the right person for this job. I need dependability, not stupidity, Mr. Busco."

"Just kidding, Ms. Sage," I said. "I'm smart, reliable, funny, and even a little daring. Everything women say they want in men, right?"

There wasn't a reply, just a sigh of relief piercing the passenger side of the car. Pixy loosened the grip on the case she clutched and fumbled for a pack of cigarettes. I motioned to the slim, white stick soon quivering between her lips.

"I have two favorite kinds of clients, Ms. Sage: those who pay and those who are alive to pay," I teased. "And I'm sorry to say you may not fit in either group because you lose a minute off of your life with each puff of one of those things."

"That study's outdated, Mr. Busco. More recent data indicate that…"

Lightheartedness seemed lost on Pixy. It was no doubt contained by the gravity of the case she carried. "Well, let's get down to business, Ms. Sage,"

I said. "For what am I risking life, liberty, and the pursuit of more property?"

Pixy's face brightened through the cigarette smoke. "A revolutionary invention," she answered. "I couldn't risk telling you over the phone or meeting you in your office or in any other stationary location because what I possess is so sought-after that…"

"Uh, what *is* it?" I tried to nudge from Pixy.

"It's a marvelous invention called sentient steel."

"Sentient?"

"I know it's a big word, Mr. Busco," Pixy admitted.

I defended my intelligence. "I know what it means," I quickly replied: "*to be conscious,* basically. But metal having a mind, Ms. Sage?"

"It fits perfectly, Mr. Busco. Sentient steel is an alloy that has aluminum's lightweightness, rubber's elasticity, and titanium's durability. With these qualities, it can be shaped into almost any form. It's like it can be metal or rubber or some other substance *it* chooses – like it can think and become. But what I need you to do is to deliver it by tomorrow evening to an address in Santa Fe, New Mexico, where I will be waiting."

I had to keep myself from laughing aloud at what seemed like overpayment for the job Pixy wanted me to do. *Two thousand and some odd dollars to deliver steel!* I'd heard of flexible metal before. Recently, I saw the stuff used in eyeglass frames. For a long time, I'd suspected magicians used something like it when they claimed to bend silverware or when the guy at the carnival bent chains with his teeth.

So naturally, my first thought about sentient steel was it was probably just an upgraded version of flex metal that Pixy was guarding. Maybe sentient steel was simply an entry into a science fair by an anxious coed with nothing to lose but a good grade or scholarship if it arrived late. Or possibly, it was a company invention or patent that she didn't want competitors to discover.

Either way, two thousand, five hundred was overpayment. But I didn't tell her. I couldn't (not in my sorry economic state). Her $2,500 – or more like $2,000 after gas, food, and lodging – would be just enough to get me out of debt.

So, I confidently eased back in my bucket seat and let sentient steel silently roll off my tongue, while Pixy spun a string of sentient steel statistics more complex than Oriental tapestry off hers. But the string snagged when Pixy shrieked, "Someone's following us!"

Yeah, several dozens or so of some bodies, kid: we're on a freeway! I wanted to say. But I saw what Pixy meant when from the traffic tore a taxi, but no ordinary taxi. This one was hailing me (only with a barrage of bumper to bumper honks and high-beams). And when I saw what looked like an arm moving out the passenger side window, I thought it might be an attempt at a drive-by shooting. *Gator Grimes's guys?* I first thought.

Maybe word hadn't got around to Gator's other collectors that Sully and Ziggy already stopped to see me. Or maybe Sully and Ziggy thought I was skipping town to keep from paying. Or maybe it wasn't Gator Grimes's guys at all. So, I sped up.

Quickly, I spotted a way out. Up ahead, a side street surfaced! I waited for the first break in traffic. It came, but at barely over a car's length. The space was closing fast. It was time to see if Hub Wheeler's twin turbo talk and four-wheel drive performance praise of the Stealth was real or really hype.

So, I threw the shifter into high gear and gunned it! We blasted through the two cars in between, before their drivers could honk their horns in protest. The Stealth's thick posture and sturdy sides kept us hugging the highway all the way, as I made a sharp turn onto an off ramp that would have sent most cars skidding on two wheels. We slid safely down the slope and sped onto a stretch of a side street. When it came to cars, Hub knew his business all right; and I'd mind my own, from now on, instead of questioning his.

I glanced in the rearview mirror. No taxi in sight – *terrific!* But for how long?

CHAPTER SIX

Hooked Like a Halibut

"Were those friends of yours?" I asked Pixy.

"They still are, Mr. Busco," Pixy said. "And they're your friends too, now that you know about the steel."

Whew! It wasn't Gator Grimes's guys after all! Focusing on my newfound friends, I asked Pixy, "Can't these *friends* of ours give us something besides a hard time?"

"Maybe a bullet or two, if we're not careful."

"Damn," I groaned. "I was hoping for a bribe: I need the bread."

"It's probably Red-Bull," Pixy said.

"*Red-Bull?* You mean like the…," I asked.

"…*Drink?* No. I mean Harlan Red-Bull: a hideously scarred Navajo man dressed in black!"

"What a relief!" I sighed. "What chance would

we stand against a man with that endless energy drink coursing through his body?"

Pixy sounded uneasy when she added, "Red-Bull could be MIB."

This time, I hadn't a clue. *"An MIB?"* I tried to follow.

"A Man in Black," Pixy tried to explain. "They look human and harass people who have seen UFOs and…"

"The smog in this town is a bitch, Ms. Sage. So try and keep your head out of the clouds as much as possible," I kindly warned my client. "I don't want your sanity corroding before I can hear more details – *important details* – about this steel stuff."

"Very well, Mr. Busco," Pixy sighed, her balloon deflated for the time being. "Last month, I also saw a strange lady talking to Dr. Pfannenstiel at the university."

I had to barge in again. *"Whoa!* Now what kind of steel? And what university?"

"Doctor Ferris Pfannenstiel: one of PU's top researchers. You know, PU: Premier Studies University. We call it PU because we stink at partying and sports, but we're pretty unique in our scholarly aptitude. Anyway, I'm Dr. Pfannenstiel's head assistant."

"I got it," I said, "All but for how to spell Pfannenstiel; write it down, Ms. Sage. Now, what's so strange about this lady you saw talking to Pfannenstiel?"

"She's tall and has long, black hair and tan skin. That could make her Native American, Latin American, Mediterranean, or maybe even Middle Eastern. The lady also wore an expensive-looking black business suit. She just didn't look like a college student, Mr. Busco," Pixy said. "Anyway, Doctor Pfannenstiel said she wasn't anyone to worry about. But I could tell that the subject troubled him."

From the sounds of it, Pfannenstiel's sentient steel afforded him a fashion model. Or maybe it was another hanger-on or blackmailer. For the time being, I mentally filed her under LIB (lady in black), figuring she was in cahoots with the man in black, Red-Bull.

Pixy added that, "So far, Mr. Busco, only four people know about sentient steel."

"Correction, Ms. Sage," I broke in. "By my count there is at least a fifth person in-the-know: me."

"Sorry, I guess I was subconsciously trying to spare you more danger."

"In this business, danger's unpredictable. It's like a Midwest wind: sometimes it's as unwelcome as a tornado; but other times, it's a refreshing breeze that eases the old ennui," I said.

Pixy's eyes lit-up. "Oh, *parlez vous francais*?" she asked me.

"Come again?" I asked.

"The word 'ennui': it's French. It means the usual, routine, boredom."

"*Oh*. Well, I heard it in "I Get a Kick out of You": an old Cole Porter song."

"He was before my time, I'm afraid."

I laughed, "Mine, too, Ms. Sage."

"I knew about 'ennui' because I speak French and Spanish. I'm learning a little Russian too, Mr. Busco," Pixy said.

I tried to steer Pixy back on track. "Getting back to your 'trying to spare me danger,' Ms. Sage. You're asking for it in spades, carrying the steel around with you."

"Not at all because the case I'm carrying is a decoy," Pixy answered. I heard her flip the latches. The case opened but instead of steel, Pixy removed a thick manila envelope. "Inside," she said, "is your airplane ticket and…"

I stopped her. "Wait a minute, Ms. Sage. If this steel stuff's all the rage, I should get it to Santa Fe in the most hidden way possible."

"Like by sports car, Mr. Busco?" Pixy injected.

"You got me there," I confessed. "But my clunker of a car wouldn't have got your case *there*."

Pixy tried to sell me on the idea that "Flying is the quickest, safest way."

But I wasn't buying it. I explained, "Airports are tricky. All the security – the dogs, the metal detectors – would pick the steel off in no time. Airports are also big. The best security is usually inside – at or near terminals. Not outside.

"Outside, they rely heavily on cameras. Thugs like this character Red-Bull aren't scared of cameras because they can't see every angle, especially at night. And they are easy to put out of action with a well-thrown rock or well-aimed bullet. The result: Red-Bull watches and waits in the shadows and jumps me before I get inside."

"Then just how do you plan on getting to Santa Fe, Mr. Busco?" Pixy asked.

"By bus or train," I answered. "For starters, their stations are smaller, which means you can see your surroundings better. Second, their security is slack: They hardly ever inspect luggage as closely as the airports do, if at all."

Pixy pounded her forehead. "Why didn't I think of that?"

"Because you have enough on your mind," I said. "I'll handle the transportation out of town. Now, what else's in the envelope?"

"Your payment: Twenty-five hundred dollars – in hundreds – as well as the Santa Fe address and a locker combination."

"Take twelve hundred and fifty back," I instructed.

Pixy was confused. *"What?"*

"Half now and half on delivery: that's how a job like this works. That way, I won't take the money and not deliver." Pixy nodded and divvied up the dough. When she was done, I asked for the scoop on the locker combination.

"The steel is hidden in a less obvious case at the Atlas Club. I work-out there," Pixy told me. She then crossed her leg. I caught a glimpse of a generous slice of smooth thigh whose pale whiteness looked lunar in the dimness. "Can't you tell, Sonny?"

Smelling of smoke, lingering liquor, and now sexual innuendo, the car could have qualified for a strip joint license. I chuckled, "Sentient steel, Pfannenstiel, and now thighs of steel? Relax, Ms. Sage: I'm hooked like a halibut!"

Pixy quickly straightened her legs and skirt. She asked me to forgive her, blaming it on stress.

"No harm done," I reassured Pixy. "At the risk of sounding ungrateful for the work, what put you on to me anyway? Why not simply call the cops?"

"You need proof before the authorities can act," Pixy said. "All I have is an empty case that a mysterious man wants. But he really doesn't want the empty case: he wants one that looks like it, with a metal inside that few people have heard of. See what I mean, Mr. Busco?"

"Clearly, for once. But what about your doctor friend, Pfannenstiel: Surely he could confirm your story to the cops, couldn't he?"

"Red-Bull threatened him if he involved the law. But Dr. Pfannenstiel didn't think Red-Bull knew about me. So he told me to take the steel to

Santa Fe for a confidant to hide. But when Red-Bull came after me, I assumed he got to Dr. Pfannenstiel and…"

I heard a sniffle and saw Pixy forcing back tears. I figured that meant there was one less person who knew about sentient steel.

Pixy regained her self-control and said, "That's why I hired you: more as a bodyguard than as a detective."

Not guard duty again! I moaned to myself. I didn't let on that I loathed it (or that I wasn't particularly dressed for it). Instead, I continued to play it straight. I asked Pixy, "Well, now I know *why* you hired me. But I'm still curious: why *me*?"

"Your name," Pixy answered me: "*Sonny*: the kind of disposition I'd hoped for."

"Cute," I answered, "but it still smells like snake oil, Ms. Sage."

"*Snake oil?*" Pixy asked.

"Uh, a whopper, a whale-of-a-tale, a…"

"You mean a lie, Sonny?"

I lightened my tone a little and laughed, "Only a little white one."

Pixy took it back. "Sorry," she said. "Truthfully, I went through the phone book and noticed you're one of the few solo private investigators listed – I mean one who is not part of a big agency. The bigger the agency, the more people there are for Harlan Red-Bull to get to and corrupt."

"Ever heard of strength in numbers, Ms. Sage?"

"Maybe I couldn't afford the big agencies' big prices, too."

"Good point."

"But more than anything, alphabetically speaking, you're in the top; so, that's where I started."

That sounded better, but I wanted more. "So, reputation never entered the picture?"

Pixy sighed, "Isn't $2,500 cash enough to soothe your wounded sense of self?"

"It's not about ego," I said. "If this steel's the real deal, it could be worth a small fortune. I'd want the best protection, wouldn't you, Ms. Sage?"

"Time for reading resumés is a luxury I can't afford. Anyway, Dr. Pfannenstiel felt – feels, I mean – the world isn't ready for the steel. I must agree. Look at how it's affecting the actions of the few people who know about it."

I couldn't believe it! All the hassle to hustle the steel out of town so it could end up out of sight – stashed in somebody's basement and only to be revealed when the world sang in perfect harmony?

"So the steel goes to Santa Fe…just to sit?" I asked.

"And you with it: that's the deal," Pixy reaffirmed the terms. "Think of the steel as money going into the bank, Mr. Busco. It will draw better interest contained, than the criminal kind of interest it's drawing in the open."

I wasn't going to change her mind and decided that at my age, I shouldn't waste precious energy trying. Instead I glanced at my client and laughed, "I guess I was wrong about you, Pixy: you have a good head on your shoulders, besides the one that's visible."

For the first time, Pixy's face softened. Red replaced the paleness in her complexion and a smile seeped from a face that was mostly fright-filled. But a screech of burning tire rubber and a rearview flash of familiar yellow refilled Pixy with panic and my foot with lead. The terrible taxi was back on our tail!

We burst past the last block, only to plunge (taxi in tow) back into traffic. It would be slow-going again (a perfect pace for the taxi to continue its terror). *Whoa!* I was so tuned into the taxi that I didn't see the stoplight that appeared from seemingly nowhere. I slammed on the brakes, avoiding one collision. But I couldn't prevent another, as Pixy's lips without warning smashed into mine.

When they unglued, I asked the reason for the clumsy kiss. "Stress again, Pixy?"

"Thanks…again," Pixy answered, breathlessly. The passenger door opened.

"Where are you…?"

Before I could finish asking, Pixy was out of the Stealth and back in the street. "I'll try to fool Red-Bull. See you in Santa Fe, and stay safe, Sonny!" I heard her shout.

At the green light, I flew. The taxi took the bait set by Pixy and veered off after her. As I slowed down, I choked up (well, just a little). That poor kid was out to save the world in a night, but was so weighed down and so alone. Well, at least she jibed with the guy who sent her into the fray.

I didn't buy their idealistic view of sentient steel. It turned a blind eye to profiting from it. Profit should be front and center, when you're taking the risks Pixy was.

But thinking back, I guess I didn't feel too cheated. For the most part, the danger was Pixy's. This Red-Bull character knew her, not me. So far, he'd taken off after Pixy, not me. Plus, I was driving a car that wasn't mine. And last, I would soon be tucked away on a bus or train, headed for Santa Fe. So far, I was seeing everything danger threw at me. They were fastballs for sure, but I was knocking them out of the park – four for four.

Then, I got to thinking about back home's breezes: about how danger now seemed more of a refreshing gentle wind instead of a tornado. It pushed profit from Pixy's periphery to the fore, where we saw eye-to-eye on a price to keep the revolutionary alloy rolling (if only eventually to a standstill in Santa Fe).

About fifteen minutes later, I slowed at the sight of a beefy man made of bronze. His broad Greek shoulders, once gleaming, were now blemished bottle green. Yet they still managed to bear the weight of the neon-lit world that was hoisted upon them. *Atlas baby, I feel your pain,* I thought as I put the car in park.

CHAPTER SEVEN

Stopping Power

On the surface, at least, the Atlas Club seemed a clever hideout for a potentially earth-shattering alloy. On the one hand, with jocks pumping so much iron already, who'd be *sentient* about more steel? And maybe more importantly, who'd think that a wiry little geek like Pixy would set foot in a fitness center?

As for the *real* reason why Pixy chose the Atlas Club, who knew? She flew before I could ask. Whatever questions I had left would only be answered once I got sentient steel safely out of town.

First things first: I had to get the case. I entered through the club's swanky revolving door entrance and hustled down the carpeted stairway to the women's locker rooms. There were several, so it took a few minutes to find the right one. When I found it, I caught my breath and waited outside for it to clear.

The last of them finally left. *Them:* being a healthy-bodied instructor leading a flock of homely housewives who were done in and drained of their swimsuit cover dreams. I sneaked in and, after a few minutes of searching around, found Pixy's locker.

The locker was of the safe design: with the lock built into the door, instead of dangling like an ornament. I took the combination out of my inside blazer pocket and looked it over. Then I skillfully spun the lock's dial back and forth until I'd entered the entire list of numbers. Inserting my middle finger in the latch's hole and steadying my thumb and forefinger on the lever release, I lifted up. There was a confirming *click*, and the locker door opened without a hitch.

Inside was crammed with workout clothes. I noticed a snazzy sweat suit. It wasn't petite-sized. And the tennis shoes I took a gander at were 7s. Both looked a little big for Pixy. But maybe she had shed a few pounds. And women are well-known for often wearing shoes that differ in size depending on the style. Nothing out of the ordinary, I concluded.

So, I hurriedly pushed the apparel aside until at last, hidden against the back wall, I saw a single square object – a case! Keeping in mind what I was told it contained, I carefully removed the case from the locker and into the light for a closer look.

It was modest-looking all right – just like Pixy described. There were no latches to flip open – just a single key hole in the center below the handle. A key-hole which I didn't have the key to, but Pixy probably did. *Smart,* I thought at first. Then it hit me.

Maybe the sentient steel case was *too* modest, in that it along with not having frills, it was tarnished, tattered, and old. What's more, with my suit coat and slacks, I'd look suspicious carrying the beat-up old bag. In fact, I'd have probably been better off carrying Pixy's shiny metal decoy case.

A sharp-dressed man with a shiny metal con-tainer wouldn't make most people think twice (except for muggers). But as for a sharp-dressed man toting a tattered brief case? They'd think drug dealer, bagman, or bum: three professions undeni-ably common to a big city like this, but ones still largely disliked enough for someone to call the cops.

Despite the odd combination of carrier and con-tainer, I grabbed the case from the locker, slammed the door shut, and hurried upstairs. But as soon as I turned toward the exit, trouble entered through its door.

A black-as-tar trench coat drenched a towering frame that was rooted in army boots. The head was large and capped with a crew cut. A thin scar streaked from the left eye to the upper lip of the figure's long face. A face that was worn…but in the way a hunk of granite is worn: weather-beaten, but standing strong. And the figure's deep-set eyes, red-veined and volcanic, fixed an unflinching gaze directly on me. When the figure's stiletto-thin lips split, a hideous smile lunged for me. It had to have been Harlan Red-Bull: architect of the terrible taxi terror.

I tore the other direction, with Red-Bull crushing the carpet in thunderous pursuit. I barreled through a door, tumbled into the parking lot, and raced behind a row of cars. Reaching into my blazer, I drew my .357 Magnum and a deep breath. Then I bolted like lightning into the open, ready for action.

But to my surprise, there was no one to confront. *No Red-Bull!* I whipped around, fearing an ambush. But still, no Red-Bull in sight. So, I holstered my gun, collected the case – and myself – and headed for my car.

A few feet from the car, I got down on my knees and checked below the Stealth for trouble. Sometimes carjackers hide below a car and grab the driver's ankles or strike them with a pipe, disabling them before running away with the ride. But this time, fortunately, no one was hiding below.

I was about to stand when suddenly, the driver's side door opened on command – *but not my command.* A shadowy figure came clean from the car, showering itself in parking lot light.

First, the heel of a sling-back style pump firmly planted one large, but slender, foot on the pavement. A second sling-back followed suit. From there, my eyes shot up the lean lengths of legs sheathed in licorice-colored nylon that disappeared into the den of a dark-colored skirt. *It was a woman!*

A thick, black curtain of smooth-as-sable hair draped the shoulders of her business jacket. And the woman's dark, sparkling eyes and cappuccino-colored complexion betrayed what looked like an exotic blend of bloodlines. Was she Native American or Latin American? Mediterranean, Middle Eastern, or maybe even mulatto?

It didn't matter. Because when her devilishly drawn red crescent lips opened, a throaty voice breathed in crisp, clear English, *"Need a lift?"*

I recovered enough to realize my situation and said to the woman, "Wait just a minute, stranger! That's my line and my car."

But all of a sudden my mind changed when another refined frame surfaced from the Stealth because this one had significantly more stopping power than sugar and spice and everything nice. The woman was aiming a nickel-plated piece at me – a .45 caliber revolver.

"On second thought, two's a crowd. You can drive; I'll walk...but in the other direction, and fast," I said.

"Good boy! Oh, since "two's a crowd," I'll relieve you of that conversation piece you're carrying," the woman insisted.

I tried pretending I didn't know what she meant.

"You mean my gym bag?" I asked, pointing to the tattered leather brief case sitting beside me.

"Precisely," the woman purred.

"It's heavier than it looks," I cautioned her.

The woman made a pained face. "So is my gun," she whined like a little girl, the voice as pretend as her expression. There was a loud *crack!* When I lifted my head from between my legs, the woman was back inside my car. With one leg stretched out the open driver's side door, she added an arm whose hand still firmly held that .45. But it wasn't aimed in the air for a warning shot as before. This time, the .45 was fixed on me.

Her look had now toughened, and the woman said with satisfaction, "Now it's lighter." She looked at the gun again; and after that, at me. With a sinful smile she suggested, "But I think I can lighten it some more, by another bullet or two."

When her thumb eased the revolver's hammer back, I gave in. "No, no," I groaned, "you've made your point."

The woman pointed her free finger at me and said, "Give me your gun."

"Damned female intuition!" I growled, reaching into my blazer for the .357. I drew it, dropped it, and slid it across the pavement.

Keeping her .45 on me, the woman leaned a little from the driver's side and scooped up the gun. But that didn't satisfy her: next, she wanted the car keys. I reluctantly tossed them over, too. "There," I said, "I'm practically powerless."

"Precisely!" the woman said. "*Practically:* but not absolutely." Her eyes and gun dropped their sights lower, to the thing she craved most. "There's the case: give it to me."

"I thought you'd never ask," I said. "May I stand and deliver?"

The woman nodded. So I collected the case, finally stood, and got a step closer to the Stealth. "That's far enough!" the woman shouted.

I lifted the case to my waist. But it occurred to me that the woman didn't say *how* to give her the case. Since she liked to play rough, I decided to give it to her…*hard!*

I shoved the case in the direction of the driver's side door and, fearing gunfire, leaped sideways into the shadows. But instead, I heard a slam, a muffled roar, and then a screech. By the time I got to my feet, all I saw were my tail lights speeding down the street. My car beat it with the beautiful burglar!

I decided to jog my memory back to the Atlas Club for a workout.

CHAPTER EIGHT

Salvador

I bet I must have burned a half a pound of fat by lugging the bulky metro area telephone book from the Atlas Club front desk. And my fingers probably walked a mile through the many pages to the Ps. I wasn't looking for Pixy, but for her friend, Dr. Pfannenstiel, instead.

Pfannenstiel is a weird name: hopefully weird enough to belong to only a few people, I thought. I was wrong…again. Not only were there twenty-two Pfannenstiels listed, but to my shock, all twenty-two told me there wasn't a doctor in there houses. Ferris Pfannenstiel appeared to be unlisted – *damn!*

My mind raced for another avenue of approach for recovering sentient steel. Suddenly, it appeared to me, but I needed a ride. With my upfront pay salted away in the now stolen Stealth, I had just the

$58 and change in carry-around cash that I started out with. So, I divided my plan in two.

Buses are slow, but cheap, transportation. I speed-walked to the nearest stop and caught my breath. While waiting, I took off my blazer and tie and rolled my sleeves. Then I folded the jacket over my arm and hid the empty shoulder holster inside. I hoped the working-class look would keep me from being mugged (since the bus stop was in a blighted part of town). But nothing bad happened, and the bus pulled up on schedule.

I had just enough change to pay the fare without having to break my fifty and draw attention. I moved to the back of the bus for a clear view of my surroundings and settled in. There wasn't much to see. Just the mostly washed out, empty stares of the night passengers, most of whom were probably riding to a dreaded overnight shift.

Soon the lyrics from the Allman Brothers' song "Whipping Post" came to mind. At nearly 30 minutes long, it's an opera of a tune! Most of it is instrumental, but the gist of the song is about a guy who's robbed by a "mean woman." She takes his money and wrecks his new car. His losses make him feel like he's been tied up and beaten.

How fitting! Although I wanted the beautiful burglar tied to the whipping post and beaten, instead of me. Of course with my bad luck, she was probably the type who enjoyed that kind of thing.

About 15 minutes later, the bus dropped me off at my first destination: Estado Dorado's Wheel and Deal (one in a chain of popular pawnshops). It was nearly closing time when I went in, but I was warmly greeted by the owner, Salvador Khan.

Salvador (or Sal, as I call him) is a little older than me and is of mixed blood, with a full head of salt-and-pepper hair, caramel-colored skin, a thick mustache, and green eyes. The Mexican and Iranian communities rightly claim him as one of their own. But other communities want bragging rights, too. Whites see Sal as maybe having Italian or Greek roots. Blacks think he's just a mulatto trying to pass for Mexican, Iranian, or Greek. And the Asians and Jews just see Sal as a competitor (which is a wiser worry than the cosmetic concerns of the other communities).

Sal's luck doesn't stop with his looks. He has the right touch when it comes to collecting stuff, too. Crammed with all kinds of goods, Sal's vaults are as diverse as his blood. They contain the high-quality stuff, stuff that's hard to find, stuff that skirts the line between legal and illegal, and imitations of the expensive stuff that are good bargains.

When I asked to borrow a gun, Sal's bushy brow rose suspiciously. "What kind of mess are you involving me in?" was the first thing he wanted to know.

"Aiding and abetting," I said. "But if I say I copped the gun, you're off the hook."

"Maybe," Sal said. "Off one hook, only to be caught by another: the government hook, for not following the rules. You know what I mean? The waiting period for the –"

"Come on, Sal," I pleaded a little, "you know me."

"Yes," Sal 'fessed up, "I know you: like the things you bring me. Your class ring."

"*Gold* class ring," I qualified.

"Gold-plated," Sal gently reminded me. "Then there was your computer."

"What about it?"

"Full of bugs. I know the things you bring me: barely usable, barely able to sell."

"But you took them."

Sal sighed. "Yes."

"You have a heart of gold after all."

Sal chuckled, "Gold is a heavy thing to carry for long, amigo, particularly at our ages. I am happy to rid myself of too much gold, especially if it is a heart made of it!"

"Listen to you," I poked fun at the notion: "Too much gold…at our ages!"

"Believe me when I say if you have it, everyone wants you for it, not for you."

"Yeah, I guess if there's too much, you can't lug it to the bank…*alone that is*."

Sal pounded his forehead. "What can I do with you!" he asked, looking to the sky.

"I can tell you what to do *for* me, *compadre*: get me a gun, please," I repeated.

"I help you because you work hard, *amigo*. But your hard work will get you only hard time if you are caught with an illegally gotten gun. It pains me to say it, *amigo*, but you will not have the money or favors to buy bail. You will for the first time have more than barely: you will have many, many years in jail.

"So, I will ask again, what mess are you in that you must have a gun in a hurry?"

"I got this case, Sal – a big one, this time. It's guarding some goods," I said.

"Hot goods?" Sal instinctively asked.

I answered, "No, it's some lab equipment – totally legit stuff. I had to deliver it out of town, but this woman stole my car and the goods. I'm out tens of thousands!"

Sal shook his head in disbelief as he moved across the floor, beyond the display cases, and through the heavy backdoor to where the good stuff was kept: the vaults. But he reappeared moments later empty-handed. I feared all he would give me was more lecturing. *First it was Hub Wheeler; now Sal.*

"You know," Sal began, "my ex took everything from me as well – in divorce court. But I got it all back because the *puta* hocked it!"

"Well, the woman who robbed me isn't an ex," I insisted. "She stole my car, not my heart, Sal."

"She's not an ex yet. Not until you get a gun," Sal said. "Then she will be an ex: as in extinct, no? Bang, bang: no more *problema*!"

That got me laughing (the first relaxing one I'd had all night). Sal finally lifted his dark-checkered golf shirt and produced a small, sleek pistol from the waistband of his gray, polyester slacks. "Take this," he told me.

I wasn't too pleased with Sal's choice of weapon. "What is this, a .22?" I carped.

Sal told me that the gun was a .32 automatic – a model SIG P230 to be exact. "It holds eight rounds, is easy to carry, and easy to draw quickly," he assured me. "It is a favorite of the Europeans."

"I can't knock her off her feet with this!" I whined.

"Then try to use your charm," Sal snorted.

"I'm no lady-killer in that department either," I sighed. Suddenly, I remembered something. "Do you still have my .38 Colt Diamondback I pawned?"

Sal shook his head and said, "Like many of the things you brought to me, you did not buy it back. So I sold it. You will be happy to know the bullets for the gun have become so expensive to produce that the Colt Diamondback is not a practical gun to use. It is more a collector's item."

"I could have sold it myself to a gun collector," I grieved for a moment.

"Now, about this woman who robbed you," Sal said. "I do not believe you will need a .38 or a bigger gun to get back your possessions from her, Sonny."

I had to argue what seemed like a silly observation. *"What?* She had a .45, Sal!"

"She had a weapon of greater force. Think, *amigo*: her soft voice, her hair, her –"

"All right, all right, so she wasn't bad-looking, but..."

"But that is how she robbed you: she used her brains to get you to look at her body. For the most part, my friend, it is how they can get any man they choose; and how they can control any man they choose," Sal said. "But you have the same weapon."

"A soft voice and long hair?" I asked nervously.

"No, a brain. Use it! Do you remember Delilah?"

"I protected this D-list diva named Delilah once. What a drag that..."

Sal sniffed out my sarcasm. "No," he butted in before I could finish, "Delilah: of the Bible."

I laughed. "Sure, sure," I confessed. "She seduced the great Samson into telling her the secret of his strength and sold the information to his enemies, who made him a slave."

"You see, Sonny, Delilah did not need a sword or spear   just her brain – to beat Samson: a man who killed hundreds of warriors."

"I see your point, Sal," I finally admitted.

"What good are you in jail for killing this woman?

If she is a criminal, perhaps there is a reward for her capture. You could turn her in, and make more than what you lost," Sal reasoned. "Speaking of rewards, I want a cut of this case that you say is worth thousands of dollars. And return my gun unused, if possible."

I grinned. *"Keep my powder dry?"* I quoted the old shooter's line. "I'll try."

I said *adios* to Sal and shut the door on my way out. My *compadre* restored my sense of humor and obligation to my client. Not to mention adding to my armament: the .32 gave me three more bullets than the five my double-action .357 supplied. But he still couldn't stub out the burning score I had yet to settle with the beautiful burglar, whom I now decided to call Delilah.

The bus pulled up on time again. I showed the driver the roundtrip ticket I'd bought earlier and climbed on board. About twenty minutes later, I returned to the Atlas Club, ready to set the second part of my plan for recovering sentient steel into action.

CHAPTER NINE

Homework

I arrived at the Atlas Club. The bus couldn't take me to my next destination. A cab would have been ideal, but the fare would break the bank. And the subway was miles away. So, I suited up and tried to hitch a ride by pretending to be a cop. But I got no takers, just people who told me to call for backup instead. Just when things looked hopeless, it looked like help arrived. It was in the form of another woman.

This one had a roundish, fish belly–white face, bright eyes, and a plump head of finely twisted braids that were twirled into a beehive on top, with the remaining twines left to spill down her back and shoulders. A filmy, green windbreaker did little to silence the shriek of yellow-and-lavender-striped Spandex that strained to cover her curves.

The wacky-looking woman ran up to me. But instead of answering my call for help, it seemed like she was the one looking for help when she said, "You're just the man I need!" It was the woman's rendition of tonight's catchy tune, "Save Me, Sonny."

To me, braids don't look good on white folks, like blond hair doesn't look good on blacks (unless both have electric guitars and are banging in rock bands). But the fact that the woman's SUV had a flat excused her strange choice of hairstyle.

I changed the tire and when the woman asked how she could ever thank me, I asked for the ride I needed. What a bargain! I first thought. The ride only cost me dirty hands and sweat. But I was to pay a bigger price than that for this trip.

Most people cool down with water after they exercise. When I work out – and that's rarely anymore – what works for me (but not my waistline) is frozen yogurt with lo-cal chocolate syrup, lo-cal whipped cream, and a cherry on top. Despite the lo-cal claims, the cherry (full of Vitamin C) is the only healthy part.

But who unwinds after a workout with a double energy drink straight and a truth drug chaser? Zinnia Prattle, the big, braided broad (as Joey DiFatino would say). I got her nickname, "Zen," and her favorite position – yoga position, I mean – without having to ask. Not that I particularly would have cared to ask.

"I should learn more about cars – about everything, honestly," Zen continued to ramble on. "That's why I take yoga: to escape pettiness and become one with everything...except with my ex. Talk about one with everything: every excuse, every morning for why he came home late every night! When Pooch – he's my dog – didn't take to him, I should have known something was wrong. It's that extra sense dogs have. Like when I lost fifteen pounds, Pooch noticed! His barks were higher pitched. I'm hoping yoga will give me that extra sense, too.

"I shouldn't ask this, but how do you think I look – I mean, for my age?"

"If I was a dog, my tail and tongue would wag," I answered Zen, dryly.

"How cute!" Zen squealed. She still lacked ESP (extra sarcasm perception that is). *"But you didn't ask me my age."*

"Well, you know what they say: a gentleman never asks and a lady never tells."

That got Zen grinning from ear to ear. She said, "Oooh, you're strong, silent and funny!"

But I got no money, honey, I thought to myself. I always held back that card, in case the chick that I didn't want wanted me. Of course lately, "no money" wasn't just an escape clause: it was the god-awful truth.

After about ten miles, my destination appeared.

It sprawled over rolling hillside and looked like a small town, with its many classroom buildings and high-rise dorms aglow, and giddy coeds hurrying to and fro. It was Premier Studies University (or PU, as Pixy called it). We parked.

I left the SUV, and Zen asked where I was going. "To do what I should have," I answered, "my homework."

Stress gets me pining for the past: for another chance to do it all over again. I was in the middle of a mess: a case where I'd lost my client's merchandise and was now scrambling to get it back. PU's campus brought back memories of my pre-P.I. existence – back in the '70s, during my college days.

Back then was really when I should have done my homework. Everybody told me I could have been a bean counter or a shrink. But they didn't tell me about the cost of college; when the money ran low, so did my patience. And I didn't finish.

In the late '70s and throughout the '80s, private investigation was the rave...*on TV, anyway.* P.I.'s belted the bad guys, bedded the girls, and bagged a hefty fee for their services – all within an hour (or about 40 minutes, minus the commercials). So, I planned to become a peeper.

What I didn't know was the best P.I.'s tend to be ex-cops, insurance investigators, and litigators. Their investigative backgrounds give them the resources to hit the ground running. As for me, I got my license through a correspondence course. Because of that, I've supported my career with crappy second jobs. Suddenly, those jobs got me thinking.

The street cred and contacts cops and investigators often gained by risking their lives I got fairly easily by working dead-end jobs. Just like law enforcers, I saw the seamy side of life and what desperation and despair lead people to do. I had some of the prosperous P.I.'s' wherewithal after all! That made me feel more confident, and I refocused on how to use my skill to secure sentient steel (whose consecutive S's looked more and more like dollar signs). But finding sentient steel meant first finding Pfannenstiel.

Pixy thought Harlan Red-Bull eighty-sixed the doc. But if Dr. Pfannenstiel wasn't dead, what would I do once I found him? Ask politely, do you have more steel to replace the steel I lost. *Nah!* I'd say I was hired to deliver sentient steel, but that Pixy didn't say where it was. That was a lie, of course.

But if Pfannenstiel was as smart as Pixy made it sound, he let her plan the whole deal. That way, if the doctor was caught, neither Red-Bull nor his accomplice Delilah could get the real plan because Pfannenstiel wouldn't know it.

But Pixy sounded loyal to the doctor. Such loyalty may have led her to disclose everything to him. The worst case scenario was Pfannenstiel cooked up the whole escape to Santa Fe and Pixy was just carrying it out. If Red-Bull got the doc, he got the plan. And of course, Delilah already got the case. And since both found me at the Club, maybe they already found Pixy and....

Analysis began to paralyze me with fear. So I quit thinking and just proceeded with trying to find Dr. Pfannenstiel.

I climbed the stairs from the parking lot to a narrow street. I crossed and traveled the length of a well-lit pathway lined with saplings to the four-story science building. A bulletin board in the lobby listed the science faculty and their office numbers. Sure enough, listed was Dr. Ferris Pfannenstiel.

The elevator dropped me off at the second floor. While the halls were empty, some lecture room doors were open. And the sharp smell of disinfectant meant janitors were around. I didn't want to dispense a bribe or a bullet, fearing I'd need plenty of both down the line. So, I adjusted my blazer and tie and prepared to pose as a dean or a professor, should someone confront me.

Luckily, I arrived at Suite FES2 without trouble. Just as I figured, the offices were all closed. But I wasn't looking to get into Pfannenstiel's office, only to his door. A professor's door is usually a billboard that broadcasts names, numbers – any way to get in touch. Pfannenstiel's door was no exception, full of sign-in, sign-out, and sign-up stuff.

I still didn't find the doctor's number, but I

found one that posed a possible lead. It belonged to Haji Savante, a teaching assistant. He was the contact for the 411 on some test scores. I rang the t.a. from a nearby pay phone.

Haji took his appointment as guardian of the grades seriously. He was the first roadblock I'd run into on campus. When I couldn't produce a name or social security number that would satisfy the t.a., I asked if Pfannenstiel had any science club meetings at his place.

That at least got the t.a. laughing. "I don't know how he does it," the t.a. said, "but for a prof, Dr. P has some serious jack. 'His place' is in a neighborhood that is as exclusive as he is."

I'd tapped into more than I thought I would! I pushed Haji for the address. There was a long pause before the t.a. replied, "I will tell you."

But another longer pause pushed my patience for the information, leading me to not so politely ask, *"Well, where is it?"*

"Meet me at the campus library," Haji told me.

"Come on!" I protested. "I just want…"

"And I just want something in return for telling you where Dr. P lives," Haji reasoned. "I am just a poor college kid. A donation could help me buy school supplies."

School supplies, my ass! I thought. More than likely, Haji was haggling for funds for a keg and chips for his next frat party. But I needed Pfannenstiel's address. "Okay, okay," I moaned, agreeing to his demand.

Haji told me to meet him in an hour. "That way," he explained, "if you're not on campus, you will have time to arrive here."

I slammed the receiver down. There were other ways of finding Pfannenstiel, but this seemed the quickest. I hurried back to the SUV. Zen greeted me with a big smile. "Howdy, stranger!" she said.

"Zen," I began to say, "I've got a student to see in…"

Zen cut me off. "You're a professor!" she yowled, like a kid who'd won a raffle.

I squirmed. *Just great!* I cursed my bad luck. "Uh, I'm retired – just a tutor, now," I finished my fib. "It's in an hour – my session, that is. I wanted you to know so when you're sitting here…"

"*Sitting here?* If it's in an hour, let's grab dinner!" Zen suggested, grabbing for the car door first.

"But sitting here alone…you could meditate better" was my try to get out of it.

But it failed. "Oh, how sweet," Zen gushed. "But we could get to know each other better over dinner. That way, I wouldn't be breaking mom's old rule 'never pick up strangers.'" I wished Zen's mom had also schooled her on the rule about not talking to strangers, too.

The PU student union cafeteria has two roomy levels. Zen chose the upper and cleared the spiral stairwell quickly for a woman her size. So quickly that she beat my elevator ride up!

Once there, we got a table and (when the student cooks got around to fixing it) our food. Zen grazed on a salad, all the while warning me of the health hazards my low-priced can of pop and slice of pepperoni pizza posed.

As dinner dragged on, I longed for my wristwatch to speed up. Maybe if it was digital – the kind that had a built-in stopwatch – agonizing situations like these might speed by second-by-second. Instead, I was stuck with my stylish, but slow, leather-banded analog ticker. But the hands finally reached eight, and I quickly excused myself for the campus library.

CHAPTER TEN

Beam Me Up

Premier Studies University is built on and around several hills. And the PU library sits on the highest hill, apart from the other campus buildings. It's newly built but looks more like one of those trendy art museums back in town, with its four brightly lit, open-glassed stories that reveal hundreds of shelves of books and tens of students studying.

The quickest way to the library from the student union is to take a series of narrow, rolling footpaths. While the footpaths are lit on either side by tall fluorescent lamps, they are lined with fully grown trees (which were probably saplings when the campus was first laid out decades ago). And at night, the foliage diminishes the lamplight. So, I discreetly drew my .32 from my jacket and started toward the library.

The walk was a lonely one. My pace was brisk.

And all the way, I cursed the small caliber of my gun. Could it possibly kill what I feared lurked in the dim, leafy boughs? Luckily, there was no holdup and I finished the hike without a hitch.

Once safely inside the library, I went to the checkout desk and asked the student librarian on duty to page Haji Savante. While I waited, I leafed through some returned magazines. *Vogue, Esquire,* and even *Maxim* were mixed in with the usual professional journals and bland bulletins. Another definite difference in college life from when I attended!

Suddenly, I felt a tug on the back of my jacket and turned. I saw a skinny, East Indian kid with medium-brown skin and straight black hair. He wore a red-striped rugby shirt that was a little too big, a pair of dark green cargo pants, and sandals. The East Indian asked if I could spare a dollar, and his reason for asking sounded familiar. "You look like you have some serious jack, with your coat and tie," he said.

"A doctor named 'P' invited me for tea. He said we dress, but didn't give me the address," I said.

"How careless," the East Indian sympathized.

"Yes: I'm in a mess," I agreed.

"Perhaps I could be of service. I am Haji Savante, sir," the East Indian finally announced, extending his hand in friendship.

"I'm glad that's over," I said, shaking Haji's

hand. "I couldn't think of a word to rhyme with mess." Then my eyes lit up. "Talk about *stress*."

"Sir, you digress," Haji said.

"Yeah, you're right," I sighed, realizing the kid had me beaten...*again.*

We had the quiet of the library, but with the building's open-glass design, I felt we still needed privacy. So we moved to a secluded table, stuck back in the corner of the reference section. I was sick of the spy shtick, so I shelled out the fifty-dollar bill I had left and told Haji to take it or leave it.

Haji's gray eyes locked onto the image of US Grant like a rebel sniper. "That's more than I thought I'd get. Thank you!" he beamed, snatching up the big bill. "Doctor P lives in Golden View Heights."

Of course! Golden View Heights was one of the dozens of ritzy suburbs in the hills above the city. Pixy's two thousand and some odd dollar proffer plus a metal worth hundreds of thousands – where else would Pfannenstiel live?

Haji gave me the address, and then pushed away from the table. *"Hey!"* I stopped him. "I've got some more questions."

"Something I love about this country, sir, is its excess. Excessive questions mean excessive dollars," Haji remarked, extending his hand in my direction. Only the palm was raised and flat. Haji wasn't ready to shake my hand; only to shake the rest of me down.

I grinned and reached for my hip pocket, brushing back the single breast of my blazer enough to let slip the shine of my semi-automatic. That wasn't enough: Haji might think I was just a thug. So, I went through with pulling out my wallet. Only instead of forking over more payola, I flashed my P.I. license. "You're looking at some excessive jail time, unless you help me," I warned Haji.

"A policeman!" Haji concluded. His dark forehead shined with sweat.

It worked! He didn't get a good look. I took control and played the punk, pumping him for all I could. "Okay, okay," Haji stammered, "what else do you require of me, sir?"

"What's so special about Santa Fe, New Mexico?" I wanted to know. "Is it because it's remote desert – lots of real estate development? I mean, I know we used it to blow up the first atomic bomb."

"Actually, the *idea* was conceived at Los Alamos, which is less than an hour from Santa Fe. *The bomb* was detonated at Alamogordo, which is far south of Santa Fe," Haji gently corrected me. "Santa Fe is the capital of New Mexico, and is hardly isolated. It is known for turquoise, Tex-Mex..."

"That's tourist clap trap!" I cut-in. "What's there science-wise?"

"The city hosts many science conferences. And within its region are many government research sites, private technology companies, and three big military bases to guard it all. Some say it is the new Silicon Valley."

I probed deeper. "Why does Pfannenstiel trust you, kid?"

Haji sighed, "I doubt he will now. But he trusted me because I believe in real science."

"Real science?" I asked.

"Doctor P hates junk science: spaceships, ray guns – you know, *beam me up*?"

"But isn't that where the big money is: in far-out inventions?"

"Modernization is where the money is: improving existing technology. Don't re-invent the wheel, sir: add better rubber," Haji told me. "Far-out inventions often need just as far-out support systems to sustain them. You may cause unemployment in other areas and high taxes to build the required infrastructure.

"Most big government contracts and grants involve many scientists pooling their ideas. Many private companies even hire dozens of scientists to work for them. Their creations are shared over time, so new ideas and products don't destroy established ones and the economy still rolls. Someday soon, I will publish these beliefs in a newsletter."

"A newsletter?"

"Yes, sir. For a mere $20 a month, students and faculty can learn about the latest developments in technology and how to invest wisely in them. It is such a small price to pay for what could be a great return. Someday, I will do this. But currently, I must concentrate on my campaign."

"Campaign?"

"Yes, for club treasurer, sir."

Haji's entrepreneurial spirit was admirable, if naive. I doubted the average student had a mere 20 bucks to invest on anything other than beer and buying stock in a good ghostwriter for term papers. And members of the faculty were probably cranking out their own more learned newsletters to those in positions of power beyond PU. I asked Haji about the club he was in.

Haji's chin raised. "I am a proud member of the techno-ethics club, sir," he said. "Doctor P is the sponsor and Premier Studies University's most respected techno-ethical Transhumanist. I have – or had – his endorsement for my candidacy as treasurer."

I was really in a daze with that disclosure. *"Trans-techno-what?"* I asked.

"Sorry. Transhumanism is merely the belief that technology is the best way to enhance the human mind and body to higher, more perfect levels," Haji said.

"Sounds like junk science to me, Haji. Doesn't that go against all that modernization jazz?"

"Not at all, sir," Haji said. "Because techno-ethics is a branch of Transhumanism: like Catholicism and Protestantism are different branches of Christianity.

Techno-ethics seeks to protect against the irresponsible and rash use of technology. A pure Transhumanist throws caution to the wind and accepts any scientific advancement without examining the costs. As techno-ethicists, we advocate cautious progress, sir."

Suddenly, the name sentient steel made sense after all. I remembered thinking how silly a metal with a mind sounded when Pixy first described it. But now, it made more sense. It wasn't a thinking metal but a metal whose design and purpose were well-thought out. And it gave me another possible lead.

Haji jumped up. "No more questions!" he told me. "I know my rights: you cannot continue to question me without the presence of a lawyer. And I'm going to my dorm to call a law student!"

Haji sideswiped some heavy books into my lap and darted like a rabbit. I tripped trying to catch up, which gave the college kid a leg up on me. I got to the main entrance hall and then raced outside. No Haji in sight – just campus buildings, aglow with neon night light. Well, at least the kid put me on to my next lead: the techno-ethics club. So, I forgot about trying to find Haji and ran back in the library.

The librarian logged me on a computer and I crammed as much memory metal stuff as I could from a Wikipedia search. Next, I got the low-down on the techno-ethics club from the list of campus student organizations. The president was a freshman coed named Bambi Wiles, and her contact number was listed.

I asked if I could use the desk phone. The librarian was a nicer kid than Haji. She said "sure thing" and didn't charge me for it. I got Bambi in her dorm. Using some of the facts and figures from my memory metals research, I fed her some flimflam about wanting to join the club. And I was pleasantly surprised when Bambi told me to stop by her dorm room for the sign-up stuff.

For a moment, my single-minded search for sentient steel sidetracked. And my old man's mind took the wheel and swerved straight into sinful city. *I was invited to a coed named Bambi's dorm room after dark!* Then, I became focused again when it occurred to me that Bambi probably looked like Pixy, but was hiding her nerdiness with a sexy name.

CHAPTER ELEVEN

Underhanded Hooey

I arrived at Bambi Wiles' high-rise dormitory around a quarter 'til nine and piggy-backed through the security locked door courtesy of some drunken students who held it open. I took the elevator up to the fourth floor and arrived at Bambi's door. After three knocks, the door finally opened. So did my mouth...*in awe at what I saw standing before me.*

There didn't appear to be anything nerdy about Bambi at all. She was of average female height – 5'3"or 5'4". But that's where average said so-long. Bambi looked to be barely twenty. I could have spanned her waist with my forefinger and thumb. But her boobs looked to be an armload: cannonballs that just about burst her clearly too tiny T-shirt. *Not that I offered her the extra large fit of my undershirt to restore modesty.* Long, obviously blonde, hair flowed from a heart-shaped face that was flawless porcelain and further beautified by big lashes that shaded a pair of swimming pool–blue eyes.

"Hi'ya," was how Bambi greeted me.

"Uh, hi there," I sputtered. "Are you Ms. Wiles: techno-ethics club president?"

"Sure am. You're the guy who wants to join up, right?"

"Yes, Ms. Wiles."

"*Aw*, just call me Bambi. All my friends call me Bambi. Come on in."

Bambi trotted back inside and I entered, closing the door behind me. "Make yourself at home, Mr....?"

I came up with another cover, off-the-cuff. "My friends call me...*Tony*," I lied. "Like the tiger."

"What tiger?" Bambi asked.

Referencing the old Kellogg's Frosted Flakes mascot really showed my age, not that Bambi seemed to notice or care.

"Mind if I call you *Tone*? I mean, there used to be a rapper called Tone Loc: I loved his stuff. I wonder whatever happened to him? Probably shot, like Tupac."

I said to myself, Tone Loc's career was dead before you were born, Bambi! And you were barely two or three when folks were tearin' up Tupac Shakur's "Thug Life" tragedies.

"Oh, I'm not saying this because you're black.

About twenty of our sixty-some club members are minorities, too. And most of them aren't into gangsta rap. I'll bet you're not. You probably groove to Michael Jackson, right?"

"*The Jackson Five*," I replied.

"Wow, old school!" Bambi beamed. I shuddered at the reminder of my age. "Oh, I hope I didn't 'dis you with that *old school* stuff. We could sure use more non-traditional students in our club, ya know."

"Of course," I said, "that's why I sped my mobility scooter over."

"Oh, I'm sorry. I'll go get the sign-up stuff!"

I took a seat in the living room and looked around the dorm room. "You've got this place fixed up real nice, Bambi," I said. "Some spread: a big screen TV, stereo, vinyl couch…"

"Leather," Bambi called from another room.

"Sorry – *leather* couch."

"Want something to drink? Like beer?" I heard Bambi holler.

Beer, I silently added to my mental inventory of things that made the coed's dorm so impressive. "Uh, no thanks, Bambi," I declined her offer. "You must have very generous parents."

"Not even," was all Bambi said about that. She pranced barefoot back into the living room with some papers in hand and plopped herself on the couch.

I pressed on. "Well then, a great job got you this setup," I said.

Bambi shook her head no, and leaned over to hand me the sign-up sheets.

"Oh well. It's none of my business how you got it, *but you certainly got it, girl!* More than I had back when I was in college."

Bambi's button nose wrinkled. "You're not in college?" she asked.

I began shaking off the charade. "Uh, not exactly, Bambi," I said, setting the sign-up stuff aside.

Bambi broke into a high-watt smile. "Well, that's okay!" she said. "I don't think anyone will care. After all, you must already have a PhD or something: with all that stuff you told me over the phone about memory metals."

"I have plenty of PhD, if you mean being piled high in debt," I replied.

Bambi slapped her knee and giggled, "You're totally off the chain, Tone!"

Then I became more serious. "I'm a friend of Dr. Pfannenstiel's."

There was a slight change in Bambi's care-free manner. "How is he?" she asked.

"Shouldn't he be okay? He sponsors the club, right? And you being the club president, I thought you two would be – how do they say it nowadays – *tight.*"

"Well, yes...yes, we are. But he doesn't come to every club meeting, you know. He's a busy, busy man, Tone. Like the meeting last week, he didn't show."

I dug deeper. "Do you know a Pixy Sage?"

Bambi squirmed on the couch. "Yes, she's our club secretary. Why?"

Bambi wasn't going to be a tough nut to crack, so I got to it. "Forgive me for saying this, Bambi, but it sounds like there's something you're not telling me. You see, the reason I asked about Dr. P is because no one's seen him in a while. Pixy asked me to kind of check up on him."

Bambi seemed to perk-up at the prospect that Pfannenstiel might be okay. "Oh, that's nice of her. She's sweet, for an art major. You know, I think we were switched at birth, Tone. With my taste, I should be into art."

"The interior decorating side, for sure," I muttered.

"Pixy should have been president of the techno-ethics club, with her brains."

Pixy, an art major? That didn't figure. Pixy was bright all right. But why would a concrete, nuts-and-bolts guy like Pfannenstiel have as his Girl Friday someone from what's typically an abstract, subtle major? Maybe it was to throw Red-Bull and the Delilah off track by not picking someone with a sci-entific mindset?

"Pixy got me to run for president, even though I'm a freshman," Bambi added.

"Why did she want a freshman to run for such an important campus club?"

"Well, I-I had this idea, see. I used to work in a

homeless shelter – as part of my community service. I got busted in high school for making and blowing bongs."

"*Marijuana – really?*"

"Yeah, I know. I don't look like the type who'd blow."

Not a bong, I said to myself. Bambi really stepped into one, but I concealed a sarcastic remark and instead said, "Just don't blow your future: stay in school, Bambi."

"That would make a great ad campaign!" Bambi said. "Anyway, Tone, I got to thinking: a lot of druggies have lab equipment that they're using to make drugs. Why not get them to use it for environmental research and inventions. We could give them scholarships to make real green, instead of the other kind of green. I'm trying to make that into a TV ad or something."

Oh my god! I actually thought this chick was irresistible just a few minutes ago. What in the hell did Pixy see in promoting her to club president?

"Has Pixy shown up for any club meetings lately?" I asked.

"Well, no," was Bambi's reply. "Is she missing, too?"

"No. Like I said, she asked me to check in on Dr. P."

Bambi sprang from the couch and ran over to where I sat. "Well, I –I've wanted to tell someone about all of this for so long," Bambi said.

"About what?" I asked, curiously.

"Pixy was afraid of something – someone."

"Really?"

"For real, for real! She had me hide something – a case. I hid it for her at a health club where I work out at."

That fit! The larger-sized athletic clothing in the locker was Bambi's, not Pixy's.

Bambi asked, "Is that what's getting her in trouble: that case?"

I tried to brush off the coed's concern. "Now who said she's in…?"

But Bambi finally homed in on some of my underhanded hooey. "I know I'm not the sharpest knife in the drawer, but I'm still a knife," she said. Then Bambi's head turned and her face scrunched up – like something smelled. She tapped her lips. "That doesn't sound right," she concluded about her knife comparison.

"I know what you mean: you don't like being patronized," I said to her softly. "Sorry I talked down to you."

"Aw, you don't have to apologize. I should apologize: for not telling you everything about Dr. P and Pixy."

"You haven't told me *everything* yet, Bambi."

"Oh, yeah, maybe I forgot some things. Well, can I meet you back here at about nine-thirty? I didn't expect signing you up to take so long. I forgot to return some books to the library before it closes."

"Why don't I tag along? We can talk over there, instead."

"Awesome, Tone!"

I had eight bucks to my name, but I felt like a million. It was like another shot of that Skyview Lounge bourbon-and-sunset brew going down. A little trickery got me the ride I needed. The fifty I gave Haji got me the doctor's address. And doubling down on deception got me more on Pixy and Pfannenstiel from Bambi.

So far, Bambi was confirming everything Pixy told me: about her fears, the case, and the threats to Pfannenstiel. But why Pixy would trust someone as ditzy as Bambi Wiles to run a club and, more importantly, with something as big as sentient steel still puzzled me. Oh well, I hoped I could continue to coax it out of the coed.

Bambi slipped into some flip-flops and a pullover that matched her running shorts. She gathered her armload of books (that I considerately offered to carry). We made it outside and headed for library. But I had to ask Bambi to slow down: the in-shape student was several strides ahead, though she wore what amounted to shower shoes!

I set in early with more questioning. "Do you know a Haji Savante?" I asked.

"Sure," Bambi said. "He's in the club. He wanted to be president, but I got it."

"What is he? A freshman, sophomore, junior, or senior?"

"A junior," Bambi answered. "He was the vice president of the club for a while."

"How did he take to a freshman being picked over him for the top job?"

Bambi shrugged. "I guess he's okay with it," she said. "We don't kick it though because Haji rolls with high rollers. He thinks they must be all that to get so much money. Maybe he saw my dorm stuff isn't the shit and decided I wasn't fly."

It sounded like Haji was more of an opportunist than a true disciple of Pfannenstiel's philosophy. Haji didn't seem to care much about anything other than making a quick buck off me. But I had to hand it to him: he had the techno-ethics philosophy down pat and peddled it with Capitol Hill skill. The stuff about little by little rather than full speed ahead with far-out inventions that could wreck the economy sounded good, even if unrealistic. If anything, Haji was a budding politician – another con man on the make.

In an ideal world, he would make for a better club president than the bumbling Bambi Wiles. But Haji lacked Bambi's winning looks and aw-shucks manner. Those two things got Bambi the techno-ethics club presidency: the easy charm that could boost club membership and the fact that Pixy and Pfannenstiel could pull her strings easier than a huckster like Haji. Maybe that's why they approached her to help hide the case.

Then I thought, If Haji knew where Pfannenstiel lived and had his endorsement, it wasn't a stretch that he knew about the steel, too. Could that have been the reason why he first thought about a news-letter: To trumpet sentient steel? But since he sold-out the doc so quickly, Pixy must not have included him in hiding the steel. So maybe *he* hooked up with Delilah and Red-Bull and helped them deep-six the doctor for the dough he needed.

I was about to ask Bambi about it when a sharp crack suddenly split the campus calm. I flinched and then whirled around, thinking the noise came from behind us. Then there was another, but this time closer – more recognizable in tone. It was gunfire!

I hit the ground only to realize Bambi had beaten me there. I crawled over and saw her lying face up, with eyes as wide as half dollars locked open and fixed on a distant, unknowable point. Unknowable because when I looked closer, an ugly burgundy blossom blemished Bambi's chest. She would never reveal what that distant point was because Bambi Wiles was shot – *dead*.

CHAPTER TWELVE

Shadows of Doubt

Bambi had been thrown on her back, which meant the shot came from up front – ahead and along the tree-lined path. But that's where the library – where help – was. I rose, fearful at first. Then I collected myself and burst into a wild sprint along the tree-lined margins of the pathway, on course for the library.

The path lights above blurred, whirled, and cut other crazy patterns through my dizzy line of sight. I finally made out the library's bright, transparent panes a few yards ahead. I was almost there when out of nowhere the fear I fretted was lurking in the boughs made itself clear.

The fear was in the form of a man – a mast of a man. He stepped from behind a tree trunk, and one of his huge hands reached for me. A hideous scar

I'd seen before helped form a rugged, reddish sneer. *"Stop!"* Harlan Red-Bull growled. "We gotta talk." My shock was such that I forgot I had a firearm and just froze.

But the biggest shock came when Harlan Red-Bull didn't move either. I finally drew my .32 when Red-Bull toppled over. From behind the giant, a familiar, fish belly–white face surfaced. *Zen!* She flattened Red-Bull with one swing of her purse. "Nice shot!" I told her.

Zen hurried to play nurse. "Are you okay?" she finally asked me.

"No, no! Someone's been hurt!" I panted.

"Hurt?"

"Yes! Go to the SUV, now!"

"But what about you?" Zen asked.

"Never mind me! I've got to get help."

By the time I got Zen off and running, I turned and prepared to take on Red-Bull. But to my surprise, he wasn't there. He'd vanished, as he had while chasing me through the Atlas Club parking lot. I gathered my senses and rushed into the library for help.

When I came out of the upper level men's room at the library, the campus police were on the scene. And about thirty minutes later, the pros made their presence felt with the typical all sirens-blaring, firearms-drawn force.

A small crowd of mostly student onlookers

gathered, but were held back by the thin blue line as the crime scene investigators unraveled a yard's worth of yellow tape and scrounged for every speck of evidence.

When they began shooting photos of Bambi's body, my first feelings for the coed hit. It wasn't guilt, but sadness: sadness for Bambi's relatives (if she had any) and above all sadness for her naiveté. Bambi managed to get herself mixed up in the steel deal, too. And though she wasn't in as deep as me or Pixy, she shared the same risk. At least I knew the risk. I blamed Pixy for not warning her of the depth of danger she dived into.

Then again, maybe Pixy did warn Bambi. But because the coed was smoking weed and drinking beer, it probably dulled her senses. So when she'd doubled down on danger by getting wrapped up in the steel deal, it made it more likely she'd lose. For all I knew, Bambi was probably dealing dope, too (from the looks of the pricey items adorning her dorm). So I began to free myself from the sadness that swamped me, as I realized some of the blame was Bambi's, too.

Soon, the ambulance loaded up Bambi's body and drove away. And it wasn't long after that a couple of PD detectives – robbery and homicide division – took me away for some Q and A.

Instead of driving downtown for questioning, we

huddled at the campus cops' small, but surprisingly high-tech, HQ.

I doubted I'd be held as a suspect or arrested as a material witness, *if it sounded like I was cooperating.* The cops verified my P.I. license and then zeroed in on the specifics of my case.

I told them I was trying to find Dr. Pfannenstiel for my client Pixy Sage. Of course, the detectives asked why Pixy wanted to find him. I gave them a reason: that he'd missed some techno-ethics club meetings and was unlisted in the phone book – both true. Then I told them I didn't have much in the way of leads: just club officers Bambi Wiles and Haji Savante.

I whet the detectives' appetites by offering up some sacrificial suspects – *sixty-some odd techno-ethics club members, to start with!* Then, they spent a good half hour taking numerous notes on the wacky techno-ethics club setup. About Bambi's dabble with drugs. Then about my hunch that Haji could have been motivated to intimidate or out-and-out eliminate the pretty young blonde who had quickly risen to become president.

Though Red-Bull was at the scene of the crime, and nearly killed me, I couldn't positively finger him. He was likely miles away from the campus. Also, I didn't want to implicate Zen (whose chatter would only make matters worse). Haji, on the other hand, would be easy to dig up (with reams of student records for the cops to access). And the fact that I told them he ran during my questioning would make him even more of a suspect for them to find.

Next, the detectives asked how I got into the dorm without a security card. "Bambi," I lied, "let me in." Luckily, I'd overheard a campus cop tell one of the uniformed pros outside at the crime scene that the main entrance's security camera at Bambi's dorm was broken. Coupled with the fact that the kids who let me through were drunk, there wouldn't be any certifiable proof that I piggy-backed in.

Finally, the PD detectives wanted to know if I had a gun. I told them it was issued by Coast is Clear Security, but was at home. I also told them I wouldn't carry a gun on a simple missing person case, especially when it meant snooping around a college campus.

Overall, my story sounded legit, with enough believable angles to keep the cops busy. Except that I lied about the gun and left out the stuff about sentient steel, Red-Bull, and Delilah. They were conscious omissions that I kept the cops out of the loop on. Because had I offered them up, it would make me look like a suspect: like I made up such craziness to hide involvement in Bambi's murder.

But even in my own mind, I still hadn't quite put all the steel deal pieces together. Were Red-Bull and Delilah working together or not at all? And without the case, I couldn't verify that sentient steel existed without Pfannenstiel. Now, I saw why Pixy didn't call the cops about all this.

After the PD lecture about losing my license if I was lying, I was released. I'd managed to wiggle myself off the hook. My first stop was the library's upper floor men's bathroom. After relieving myself, I reached into the trash and was relieved again to find my .32 was still stashed. Though it hadn't been fired, I had ditched it to keep from being booked as a suspect, instead of being questioned as a would-be witness.

I was fairly certain that once they did Bambi's autopsy, what had to be a rifle slug would turn up. Then ballistics would show that it was impossible for me to have killed Bambi while walking alongside her. But it was still possible for the cops to believe I may have schemed to kill her. Though I hoped the show of eager cooperation I put on for the PD earned me the benefit of their doubt.

I returned to the SUV. Zen loyally waited inside. But she wasn't her bouncy, blithe self. Instead, she was visibly concerned. "I should have known," Zen started in: "The strong, silent act; the blue sport coat; and the meeting at the library. The collective was telling me all along."

"Telling you what?" I wanted to know.

"That you're a cop! You're hot on the trail of some lawbreakers, right?"

I renewed my role from outside the Atlas Club

and said, "Guilty as charged. And now that you know I'm a cop, I must ask what your role in all of this is."

"I'm not in on anything!" Zen bawled. It was the first time I'd seen her upset.

"The hell you aren't!" I shot back. "It was too convenient: You arrived on cue to deck Harlan Red-Bull and maybe you killed – I mean, hurt – that coed, too. Red-Bull probably faked being hit to fool me into feeling safe with you." I drew my .32 and swung my attention out the passenger side window. "Is he coming, Zen?"

"I never took you for a paranoid delusional! I don't know who that guy was, and I'm not working with him," Zen maintained. "I was on my way to see if you were done tutoring when I saw that tall goon coming toward you. So, I focused all my energy at one point and hit him with my purse."

Things were quiet for awhile, inside and outside the SUV. That gave me a little more time to think. Paranoia was getting the best of me. Red-Bull and Delilah had the steel, not Zen.

All of a sudden, it hit me. Maybe Zen was working with them as a simple stooge who was paid pennies up front, with no idea of the value of the steel. That's how players like Red-Bull and Delilah usually operate.

Zen could also be just a decoy. She did pick me out kind of fast outside the club and got me to waste time changing a suitably flat tire. Maybe they even thought I was horny. That all Zen's blather about being hot and bothered would get me turned on to her and off the trail of sentient steel. *Fat chance!* In fact, Zen didn't lead me off track. She got me back on it, with the ride I needed. And the fact they didn't hire some hot-looking escort or hooker to do the trick nixed the whole Zen as decoy idea.

Just when my cerebral coast cleared, another shadow of doubt clouded my judgment. Maybe Zen was a hired gun after all. And she'd be perfect: unsuspecting, in her crazy clothing and constant chatter. With my fingers in my ears, how could I pull my gun to get her? Zen could get the drop on me easily! She could pull a pistol from her purse and fulfill her contract: to pop me and keep me from talking.

But *Zen* was doing all the talking. It was only way she could kill me: by talking me to death. And man, had she come close, but not close enough for me to worry about her being part of the steel deal.

CHAPTER THIRTEEN

Vengeance Revived

"So this is their hideout," Zen seemed to gasp as we made the highway turn-off toward Golden View Heights: the alleged locale of the elusive Dr. Pfannenstiel. "You'd think criminals would want to hide in the city, but not up here," Zen continued.

"This is exactly where criminals would flock to. The rent up here's higher than the hills, meaning someone has money to pay it. And money – lots of it – is what most criminals want," I said.

"I meant that up here, everything seems clearer: the air, the view – all of it is perfect for meditation," Zen said. "Maybe that's why I think I know what I want to do with my life now. Maybe I could be a police psychic!"

"Zen," I began in what I hoped she would realize

was a serious tone, "you were helpful in beating up one of the bad guys back there, but…"

"I know, I know: police work is too dangerous, right?"

"It was luck that you saved me. Now, I'm saving you. I know that yoga stuff you told me about works wonders…"

Zen wasn't satisfied and tried to sway me with, "A psychic does most of the work at home – or, if I was a policewoman, from behind a desk. So I wouldn't…"

"Zen, that guy you knocked out is part of a bigger, deadlier operation. I misled you about a lot, but not about this. So please, stay out of it," I firmly advised her.

For the first time, Zen was down in the mouth. The ride became quiet – as if someone had died. I hoped it was Zen's immaturity that passed on.

Soon, the thicket that lined the winding road thinned and the gaudy shine of hundreds of house-lights signaled our arrival. Golden View Heights; the SUV stopped. When Zen asked if the crooks were close, I told her no: that their hideaway was still far away – that I wanted to sneak up on them on foot.

I looked over at Zen and told her, "Thanks for everything."

Zen nodded. "Thank you, too."

"For what?"

"For what it's worth, this was my most thrilling

blind date. It's not often *the girl* gets to save the guy and the day."

"Not to mention buy him dinner," I added. "I guess there's something to be said for women's lib after all: it really saves a guy!"

Zen nodded in agreement. "You know, I hoped it might work between you and me. But it doesn't look like it will, does it?"

Sadly, I shook my head. "No, it doesn't, Zen. You're a nice person, but I'm not."

"Well, happy hunting, all the same. And I hope you get those guys," she said.

I told Zen, "I hope you get some too – *nicer ones*, though."

I got out and watched Zen wave my way for the last time. Then she drove from sight. And I resumed my search for Pfannenstiel, this time through the Heights.

After about a half an hour of walking around, I approached a hilly cul-de-sac. Perched on top was a big, Mediterranean-style mansion, complete with those arching windows and doors and the famous overlapping colored tile roofing. Unlike the other residences, there were no security fences protecting it. The outside lights were off, but the creamy exterior made it stand out in the dark.

As I approached the circular, cobblestone driveway, something else stood out in the dark that shouldn't have. I remembered thinking how its sleek black finish would be perfect for late-night stake-outs and for slipping speed traps. Parked was the Dodge Stealth. Though the car was out of place, *this* was the place!

My car started me thinking. The last time its driver's side door opened, it almost turned out to be death's door. And I sensed that same angel of death who stepped out of the Stealth before was watching now – waiting for me to walk through the mansion's portico and press the front doorbell (and with it, my luck). Instead, I drew my .32 and searched for another way in.

I noticed the big front room windows. Below them were short, but thick, hedges that would make perfect cover. I crouched and crept across the hedge row until I reached a suitable stopping point. Carefully, I rose on my heels and inched my head above the leaves to the window sill. Once there, I peeked through one of the front room window's high, arching panes. Inside the mansion was pitch-dark – no sign of life. So I hunkered down again and hurried across the remaining hedges until I cleared the length of front lawn. I made it (unseen, hopefully).

I decided to make a backdoor entrance. The land leading to the back of the mansion was a grassy slope that (with any luck) led to level ground. I edged my way down the incline until I reached the flat footing of the backyard. The full moonlight above gave the grass a ghostly blue cast, and made it bright enough for me to move around. After a couple of minutes, I happened upon an empty swimming pool; and on its deck was some of that wrought-iron lawn furniture, but without cushions.

As I moved past the pool and toward the mansion, the moonlight uncovered a grayish slab – probably a patio. Above it, the glow exposed what looked like large glass doors. But like the glass windows in the front of the mansion, the large glass doors in the back were dark, too. *Damn!* Pfannenstiel wasn't home!

Now what? I thought. Then a light came on, but not the one in my head. Instead, it came from behind the large, glass doors: an artificial, low-watt flicker revealed curtains that now glowed with the color of the smoky sunset I'd seen hours before at the Skyview Lounge. Someone was home after all, but was it Pfannenstiel?

When I didn't see a shadow moving behind the curtains, I rose from the refuge of the wrought iron couch I crouched behind. Then I hurried from the swimming pool deck and back onto the grass. From there, I beat a path for the patio. There was still no movement from behind the curtains ahead. But the patio was out in the open, giving me no cover (if someone should suddenly open the glass doors).

So I dashed for what seemed to be the safety of the shadows off to the side of the doors. I got there unnoticed and stayed concealed for about five minutes. After I determined it was safe, I crept toward the side of the large glass door. Upon examination, I discovered it was of the sliding variety. Further scrutiny revealed the door was ajar!

I ran a cautious finger that wasn't my trigger finger – in case someone lay in wait behind the curtains and cut the finger off – alongside to see if the gap in the sliding door was large enough to pry open. It was! With my .32 ready in my right hand, I stuck my left hand into the crack. Gently, I nudged the door back enough to sneak a quick look inside.

The room looked like a den, but the furniture didn't seem fit for a mansion. There was a glass-topped coffee table littered with magazines in the middle of the room and two hard-backed wooden chairs on either side of it. Behind the coffee table and chairs was a black, leather couch, and beside it was an end table with a turned-off lamp. My eyes concentrated on the couch because someone was stretched out on it.

I made out something white covering its head and torso – white hair and a white coat. I couldn't get a good look because the person on the couch was backlit from, again, inadequate lighting for such a luxurious-looking place. The sole source of light gleamed from a hanging lamp with one of those mosaic glass shades – the kind that dangles over pool tables in old-style bars back in town. And the lamp dangled through a squared-out hollow in the facing wall. Through the hollow, I saw a kitchenette, with cabinets and part of a refrigerator.

Just then, there was a noise. I glimpsed a sliver of yellow light out of the corner of my eye. A door was opening inside, but I dove back into the safety of the shadows before seeing who opened it. When the patio pavement glowed brighter, I crept back to the crack in the sliding door for another peep. This time, the end table lamp was on, making the den brighter and filling out the features of person on the couch.

It was an elderly man, with long, white hair combed back. And from the look of his wrinkly, reddish-brown face, he was Native American. A white lab coat covered what was ordinary clothing: a button-up shirt, slacks, and loafers. The only thing missing was a mustache. With whiskers, the man could've passed for a tanned Albert Einstein.

Without warning, a long shadow knifed into the cheap, white carpet of the den. I barely ducked out of sight in time. Slowly, I surfaced from the shadows to see who entered.

Wrapped in a crisp, white blouse (with sleeves rolled, collar raised, and two front buttons popped); a tight and dark dish towel–sized skirt; and dark nylons that glistened as they glided down miles of legs, the beautiful burglar Delilah cut an even more striking figure than before. She was the only furnishing fit for the mansion.

So that's what happened to Pfannenstiel's furniture: the bitch crammed it in my car! I thought.

This time, I stood, boldly grabbed the side of the sliding door, and sent it rolling. The heavy, glass pane slammed against the far wall, startling Delilah. With her defenses down, I parted the sliding door curtains and stepped calmly, triumphantly into the den. My vengeance was revived.

CHAPTER FOURTEEN

Riding the Edge

Delilah regained her composure and coolly breathed, in that throaty voice that nearly knocked me out the first time I heard it, "Long time, no see."

But this time, I dodged her attempt to punch me with her prettiness. I raised my pistol, instead of dropping my jaw. Salvador Khan would be proud: I was thinking with the right head.

"You're dressed to kill, but not me...*Delilah*," I responded.

"*Oooh, a man of the cloth!*" she shrieked with derisive delight. "Well, preacher, I'd think *you* should want to be Delilah. She was smart: she got what she wanted."

"And lost it all," I replied. "Even in chains,

Samson still brought down the house – only literally in the end: on his enemies' heads."

"And his head, too. He died."

"And so will you, if you try to play me," I warned, cutting Sunday school short. "I'll lay you out cold, like your boyfriend there. You may have stolen his heart, but not mine."

"Maybe I won't win your heart or mind, but I still have your car," Delilah said, adding an innocent little girl's smile and sway that I didn't buy for a second. "If you'll let me get the keys, you can…"

"*Freeze!*" I shouted. Delilah's sling-backs stopped in their tracks. "Turn around!" I added. When she did, I set my sights on her chest. Sadly, they were gun sights.

Delilah calmly told me, "There's something more valuable for you than your car keys, if you'll let me get my wallet, Mr. Busco."

Her perfume reeked of a ruse. "Where's the wallet?" I wanted to know.

"In the kitchen," Delilah replied, pointing over her shoulder.

My lip curled. "Just where you belong," I snorted. The sexist remark finally got Delilah's expression to sour. I was happy to wound her with it (instead of with a bullet). I walked over and spun her around. "Ladies first," I insisted, sticking my .32 in the small of her back.

We moved carefully toward the kitchenette.

Once there, my eyes locked onto the black purse parked on top of the range. I nudged my captive toward it. She reached for the purse, but I sensed she was reaching too quickly. So I pressed the point of the pistol harder and deeper in her back.

"Easy does it, Delilah," I advised her.

She got the purse, and I quickly moved her back in front of me and guided her back into the den. Before she could open the purse, I snatched it. With my free hand, I undid the secured, gold-colored clasp and dumped the contents on the carpet. I looked down to see what fell and saw a virtual gun show at my feet.

Slowly, I took a knee and scooped up Delilah's nickel-plated .45. I ejected its moon clip, and threw it aside. I found my .357 and aimed it (along with the .32) at my prisoner. Then I got my car keys, but not the wallet. I feared it was booby-trapped.

So, I got up and told Delilah to get down. "You open the wallet!" I ordered.

Delilah got the wallet, flipped it open, and then basked in the sheen of a copper shield embossed with numbers. "I'm Special Federal Agent Bevel Brand," she announced.

"Federal Agent?!" I couldn't believe it. "You've got nerve, you carjacking, .45 caliber–packing…"

"When hunting for bear, you better go loaded," Bevel replied.

"With a .45?" I laughed. "Trying to bag a grizzly

with a six-shooter is like trying to eat soup with a fork!"

"A difficult, but not impossible, task," Bevel countered.

"Besides, a grizzly hasn't been spotted around these parts since they pasted the last one on the state flag," I joked.

"There are *other* kinds of bears. And the ones I'm wary of pose a threat to a community greater than a few campers," Bevel said. Then she curtseyed sarcastically and said, "Besides, try concealing a hunting rifle and scope in this outfit."

"That's what you get for dressing *GQ*, instead of G-Man," I remarked, lowering my weapons. "Style and smiles work, to a point."

An icicle-sharp smile cut across Bevel Brand's face. "Hopefully it's a dagger point, poked in the opponent's eye," she blustered. "The copy of your license I found in your car worked, to a point. It told me you're a P.I., but I need to know more, Mr. Busco."

"Well, let's see," I began, with a scratch of my head, "I'm 6'1", fly for fifty-five, and a Sagittarius... *by profession*. Unfortunately for you, I don't like women who take my car – and particularly me – for a ride."

"I was taken on quite the ride myself tonight," Bevel shot back. "And my stomach – no, my patience – wasn't up for another."

A ride, I thought. "You were the one in the taxi chase!" I quickly concluded.

"And you were the one on the run with an important item," Bevel said.

"Yes: a case," I casually admitted. "But P.I.'s and cases usually go together."

Bevel didn't seem amused, and turned her attention to the man on the couch.

I asked her, "Is he…"

Bevel shook her head "no." "He's not dead," she confirmed.

"Thanks for the diagnosis, but I meant is he who I think he is?"

I expected the female fed's response to be as fuzzy as her bear metaphor. Instead, it made sense. "He's an investment with enormous potential," Bevel replied. "Whether it is to help or to harm is unclear."

"But what about that bear you talked about? Is it on his tail?" I asked.

The female fed side-stepped the question, and moved instead toward a side door on the other end of the room. It was the door I'd detected from outside earlier. Not knowing who or what was behind it, I readied my guns again. But when one slender, leather pump after the other paved the way back into the room without escort, I relaxed.

Bevel returned carrying the case she stole from me at the Atlas Club. She must have jimmied the keyhole, because the case opened on command. Bevel then flung it to the floor. My jaw followed, hitting the floor seconds later when I finally saw what the much-sought-after satchel contained.

"Nothing," Bevel revealed. "Empty."

I was stunned. *"Empty?"* I echoed. "Then why the car chases, the…"

"You were planning on taking this to Santa Fe, weren't you?"

"Not without a clean change of clothes and a toothbrush! Seems I forgot to pack."

"You're in over your head, Mr. Busco," Bevel told me.

"That's funny. When I was a kid, they said when everything was bombed, that was the safest place to be: the old *duck and cover* routine, you see."

"So you like holes? Maybe I can offer you one," Bevel put forward. The prospect immediately aroused my interest. That was until the female fed said, "The hole is in Leavenworth. And you won't have a blast, Mr. Busco."

I put on my best poker face and smiled. *"Prison?"* I commented. "That threat is as hollow as your case, lady. In fact, that's just the kind of case you'll have in court – empty!"

"Stop it!" Bevel shouted. "I can take your freedom, license…,"

I barged in. "Take my debt, too," I begged, "so when you take my life, the RIP on my slab will mean resting in peace, and not return, interest, and principle."

The female fed collected herself and came back determined to win me over with the soft sell – a rational approach. She warned me, "That case is a lot of baggage, Mr. Busco."

I challenged the female fed. "Yeah, but it's highly valuable baggage. Like a *Prada, Gucci,* or *Dior* handbag. And whoever gets what's supposed to be in it will have the world on a sentient steel string."

Bevel's dark-brown eyes lit up just enough for me to see I'd said the magic words. I was in the game again, so the female fed finally opened the playbook. But again, what she said was a mystery. "Riding the edge is very, very risky business, Mr. Busco," Bevel breathed.

Confused, I asked Bevel, *"What edge?"*

"The cutting edge," she replied. "Dr. Ferris Pfannenstiel has tremendous ability for good, if he is supervised. If left on his own, his invention might ruin important sectors of our economy. Take the car dealers and body shops, for example. A car with a sentient steel bumper may…"

"May sell for triple the price of the average car, with the right advertising campaign, of course," I argued. Satisfied with my comeback, I said, "It's your move."

"Sentient steel virtually bends like rubber. It rebuilds any damage done to it. So if a sentient steel fender was rear-ended, it would retain its original shape without a scratch. A damaged car fender that can repair itself would negatively impact the car dealers, meaning fewer car purchases. Then, it would trickle down to the repair shops; then to car insurers..."

Still, I wasn't convinced. "The quality of metal improves over the years. I've seen memory metals reshape themselves before," I yawned.

"Have you seen memory metal not just reshape itself, but replicate itself?"

"What?"

"Nanotechnology," Bevel explained to me: "It's the science of controlling matter on a subatomic level. Doctor K. Eric Drexler extensively researched and popularized the subject. At first, engineers created microscopic machines and programmed them to do simple tasks, like arrange themselves from random letters into a word. Next, they were tasked with restoring damaged matter – like skin or metal – to its original state.

"But now Pfannenstiel's raised the stakes. He's created a machine called a molecular assembler: a device whose molecules can duplicate more of themselves. The machine works like a microscopic factory. Once enough assemblers have been re-created, they can be re-programmed to produce whatever product the programmer wants: Food, water – virtually any matter. Sentient steel is the first thing to be made by the assembler – the ultimate proof of concept, you might say."

"And is it any good?" I asked anxiously.

"I risked life and limb chasing you halfway across town in a toxic taxi, and now, to move the molecular assembler's maker out of town. So you tell me, Mr. Busco."

The assembler sounded like the bomb-diggity, as Hub Wheeler might say. The ultimate gotta-have-it gadget. Everyone would instantly want one. Of course, they'd probably replicate money and valuables with their assemblers at first. But then who'd need money when the assembler could make all the stuff you'd need money for: clothes, food, medicine, building materials for shelter. *Damn!* I really short-changed myself! I should have charged Pixy way more for this job, I thought.

Bevel's voice interrupted my train of thought. "Do you see where I'm going, Mr. Busco?" she asked softly.

"Yeah," I moaned. "And I can see where the assembler's going...in the can. I rarely buy into conspiracy crap, but now? Now, Uncle Sam's going to bury this invention. It will never exist, right?"

"I'm not saying that," Bevel protested. "Last year, over 3,000 inventions were held for *cost analysis*, Mr. Busco. It's better to thoroughly examine the assembler and its products – like sentient steel – before putting them on the market for consumers."

"Compassionate capitalism – *please!*" I grunted. "We both have metal on our minds. Only you want one pinned on your chest; I want more jingling in my pocket."

"This isn't about personal gain, Mr. Busco. It's about our country's security: first, last, and forever," Bevel argued.

This G-Woman is bringing her A-game: Lean, mean, and now keen, I thought. And for the first time she got me to see what Pixy and Pfannenstiel saw: pandemonium. Theft and murder rates alone would skyrocket, as those who couldn't afford the assembler would steal and kill for it. And taken to a political level, fanatics might talk a sympathizer with an assembler into creating bullets or bombs for them to use against their enemies.

But instead of admitting to an assumed Armageddon set-up and surrendering, I managed to stand my ground. In the here and now, what could I gain from all of this? I asked Bevel Brand. "Okay, how much is it worth?"

Bevel looked confused. "You mean the steel, Mr. Busco?" she asked.

"No, Agent Brand: I mean my promise to forget about sentient steel and Pfannenstiel – how much money?"

Bevel stomped. "It's always about Sonny Busco!" she huffed.

"It's about my pledge of allegiance to the payday

loan place, the pawn shops, and the loan sharks. And they don't deal in red, white, and blue: just the long green, of which I'm short," I replied.

"You're broke because you're too fixed on the fast buck. You know the price of everything, but not the cost of getting it," the female fed told me.

Just then I heard a creak. I turned to see yellow light leaking along the far wall. Someone was coming into the room. Before my revolver cylinders spun, I did – as in upside down. Bevel floored me with a karate kick, and before I knew it, that someone in the den joined Bevel. I finally got to see The Man in Black and The Lady in Black in concert, only I feared the song they'd sing would be the last I'd hear – a funeral hymn, *Nearer My God to Thee*.

Harlan Red-Bull's laugh was gruff. "Lady Luck's on my side now," he snarled. Then he drew a shotgun from beneath his trench coat and leveled it inches from my face. "Drop your guns or I'll drop you!"

I gave up my guns (and with them, it seemed, my life). Red-Bull took the .357 and kicked the .32 toward Bevel Brand.

"Get on your knees!" the female fed told me. I did. "Oh, this will sound familiar, I'm sure, Mr. Busco, give me the car keys, please." I did that, too. Finally, Bevel told me to put my hands behind my back.

I cursed myself. Bevel didn't get me with her body this time, but with her brains. I fell for her phony badge. *Damn!* I didn't deserve to live, but fought on. I fired my only defense – a furious look – at Bevel, wishing it could kill. "You lying…" I began to say.

Before I could finish, I felt a kind of steel that wasn't sentient, but cold and hard instead, wrap up my wrists. Red-Bull lifted me to my feet and pushed me into Bevel Brand's custody. Red-Bull then secured his shotgun below his coat, went to the couch, and scooped Pfannenstiel up. Bevel slipped back into her black business jacket and pushed me toward the sliding door. And we all exited out the back.

We got to the Stealth, where Red-Bull lay Pfannenstiel down and moved into the open driveway. I saw him draw a cell phone from his coat and speak into it. When he was finished, he turned to Bevel and me (who were behind the Stealth) and nodded.

About 10 minutes later, an automobile – a black van – appeared in the distance. It turned along the last street and raced toward the mansion's cul-de-sac road. The high beams blinded me when it swung into the driveway and screeched to a halt.

Red-Bull's silhouette hurried around the side of the van, as I heard its heavy door begin to roll open. Finally, the high beams kicked off upfront. But from the side of the van, some other bright lights rapidly came into view: intense, fiery-orange spurts. *Gunfire!* I watched Red-Bull fly backwards; and Bevel forwards, with my .32 drawn.

I was left alone with the car and Pfannenstiel –
perfect! Only I was handcuffed and unable to escape.
So, I hunkered down behind the Stealth, praying
it lived up to its name. So much for that! Before
long, a black-clad character in a ski mask stood over
me. "Get up!" he growled, threatening me with the
barrel of what looked like a submachine gun.

I did what I was told and he led me toward the
van. Once there, another ski-masked attacker jumped
out and ran past. But I didn't see Red-Bull or Bevel
Brand. Was this part of their getaway plan: faking
their deaths to throw the authorities off their trail?

We got to the van, and I was shoved into the
dark back cabin. The door slammed shut, and dark-
ness descended. I wiggled myself into a sitting position. It wasn't long before I sensed the perfumed
presence of someone else in the cabin with me.
"Bevel?" I nervously called out.

CHAPTER FIFTEEN

Bad Actor

The next sound I heard didn't come from the mysterious person sitting up front in the van's passenger cabin. Instead, it came from the van door opening. And the two attackers deposited a still lifeless-looking Pfannenstiel almost in my lap and jumped in.

The ignition snarled to life. But being handcuffed, I couldn't ready myself. I was thrown backward as the van rapidly reversed; and then forward, when it whirled around and sped off. Between tossing and turning, I hit my head on the floor and was knocked out.

I was awakened by a cold, firm sensation (which turned out to be a floor). This was followed by a cold, damp sensation (which turned out to be a splash of water). I slowly rolled from my stomach onto my back and realized the handcuffs were gone too. I rubbed my eyes. But when my focus sharpened, I saw I was still in trouble.

Two pale-white men dressed in black (from their army boots to their turtlenecks) stood over me. Both looked as if they'd stepped out of central casting. The taller of the two was a broad-shouldered blond. With a turned-up nose, arms folded, and a chilly, blue-eyed glint going on, all he needed was a black captain's hat and he'd have passed for a movie Nazi. The shorter guy was burly, but bald. He resembled a Russian weightlifter, with a thick neck and arms and beady eyes.

Suddenly, I heard a voice. It was womanly and worried in tone. "Is he okay?" it asked. The European-looking men backed off and a pair of nearly knee-high go-go boots hurried towards me.

"*Pixy!*" I shouted. They got you, too?" I propped myself up on my elbows before Pixy knelt and placed her hands on my shoulders, as if to calm me. "Are you okay?" I asked.

"Yes," Pixy responded softly. "But it's you who has the problem." Her hand rose; in it was my .32 automatic. "Don't do anything stupid, Sonny," Pixy warned.

She waved me up at pistol point.

I stood, but only to be grabbed by the two Europeans. Each took one of my arms and dragged me across the cold concrete floor of what appeared to be a large storeroom of a warehouse. Packing crates and boxes stacked the walls, blocking me from seeing windows, doors, or any way out. Up ahead, I saw the white glow of a light. Soon the Europeans hauled me into the intense white heat of a mega-watt, overhead lamp.

I heard the sounds of something scraping the floor. It turned out to be a hardback wooden chair. One of the Europeans dragged it below the lamp; the other plopped me in the chair. Both men backed away, leaving me to go blind in the glare. But I heard more noises, which led me to twist and turn out of the intense light to see what it was. It took my eyes a few minutes to adjust, but when my sight returned, I saw I had company.

I fixed on a slumped, seated person dressed in black – well, almost black. The legs were a mottled mess of black and a lighter color – brown, prob-ably. The brown looked like skin that was showing through black fabric. But the kicker was the per-son's feet: they were covered in scuffed, sling-backed pumps. *"Bevel?"* I called as I had in the van, only with more urgency now.

The person turned toward me. A shaky hand brushed back the long, tangled hair that hid its face. Through what looked like a bruised jaw, a husky voice answered my call this time. "Long time, no see," Bevel Brand responded.

"So, you are a fed!" I replied. "I thought you were shining me on back there, with a bogus badge."

"Looks like I've lost my luster, Mr. Busco," Bevel softly apologized, "but not my life." Bevel straightened and resolved, "They got Red-Bull, but not me…never!"

The approaching click-clack of high-heeled boots broke up my reunion with the female fed. Soon, the owner of those black patent-leathers swaggered into view. Pixy bent into the surgical-white spotlight that beamed above.

When she looked at me, her face was flushed with devilish delight. "Rinaldo Weathers, a.k.a. Sonny Busco," she remarked with the clinical cool of a coroner. Pixy's revelation of my government name – a name that called to mind dull, unmoving Midwestern memories – made me feel like a cadaver.

"Don't look so pissed, Sonny. I said I was a 'bad actor,' remember? You could've cracked your case from the start, if you had street slang skills that were up to 21st century speed. You're so September 10th: so behind the times. And now you're behind the 8-ball, you cornpone P.I.!" Pixy sneered. "Don't worry about a background check, miss. A secret catchphrase will do. But your hayseed silliness proved handy."

"Looks like we were made for each other: a dumb-ass detective and a dimwitted debutante," I replied, trying to belittle Pixy, too.

"*How romantic!* But you're already engaged, Sonny. Too bad it's to a hopeless cause," Pixy laughed some more, pointing my pistol in Bevel Brand's direction.

The female fed returned fire, swearing to Pixy, "You'll never get away with this!"

The customary warning bounced off Pixy, as if she wore a sentient steel bra beneath her blouse. Instead of that jumble of nerves that jiggled in the Stealth, Pixy was now full of nerve.

She bragged to Bevel and me, "I've already gotten away with it! We knew about your plan to move Pfannenstiel to another location. So, we stole your mission code. That gave us your passwords and communications frequencies, especially, your getaway van's transponder frequency. Right now, your back-up squad is following that signal. They think it's you: that you're returning to base with Pfannenstiel. But when they catch-up to the source of the signal, all they will find is an abandoned Dodge Stealth – minus, of course, Pfannenstiel."

"What about sentient steel?" I asked.

"You pegged it right, Sonny," Pixy replied, "It's worth a fortune!"

"*Memory metal?* Good luck selling more when there's a ton of that stuff already."

"But not metal made from a molecular assembler. Sentient steel's a sample; the assembler's where it's at, Sonny. But for all his brilliance, Pfannenstiel couldn't see past the gloom and doom of it all.

Techno-ethical research was his thing: daydreaming of a better day to make known the assembler. Easy to do, *when you already have everything!*

"Pfannenstiel was a two-faced fat cat, with his nice job, nice house, and unlimited funding. He tired of my arguments to sell the steel, which explained the appearance of our not-so-secret agent at PU. Pfannenstiel ratted me out!"

Pixy was doing such a great job of convicting herself that I decided to offer her more rope, and asked about Bambi Wiles' murder. "So, you had to silence one of Pfannenstiel's biggest supporters in the techno-ethics club president, too?" I asked.

"Supporter?" Pixy laughed. "Bambi was an idiot: an ex-cheerleader who didn't know steel from iron! I made her president so she could sweet-talk the assembler specs from Pfannenstiel. She couldn't even to do that right! So, I had her simply hide the case for me. But the ungrateful bitch wanted more than the $5,000 I gave her. Said she'd squeal, if she didn't get a bigger cut. She got a cut all right: *cut out of the picture!* Speaking of money, Sonny, guess how much I got for passing this stuff on? Try a million!"

"A million in what: travelers' checks?" I mocked.

"He's right," Bevel chimed in. "You'll never enjoy your reward stateside."

"You'll be plastered on every post office wall and TV wanted show, from Waikiki to Washington, D.C.!" I added.

Pixy shrugged. "Everything else's leaving the country anyway – companies, jobs, employers…so why not me?" she remarked uncaringly. "Happiness is now elsewhere, Sonny. I've finally bought myself the opportunity to follow it."

"Could you buy me a clue first?" I asked. "You have the steel and your hefty finder's fee. What's more to gain in kidnapping us, a captive audience, to hear you gloat?"

"We set up a sting in Santa Fe," Bevel cut in. "With Harlan Red-Bull's help…"

Pixy lost it. "That back-stabbing Red-Bull got what he deserved: a bullet!"

"Red-Bull was a concerned citizen," Bevel countered. "His interest in the steel was for a different reason – a headline. He was a reporter."

"She means an informer, Sonny," Pixy clarified the comment. "Beware of the military industrialists: they lie."

Bevel dared to grunt her disapproval. "Red-Bull told us about a border meeting between Sage and her buyer to arrange smuggling the steel out of the country. We cased the Atlas Club to confirm the courier's identity. We were to follow him to Santa Fe, catch the buyers red-handed, and collar them."

"*Bravo!*" Pixy hooted. "I hired Sonny to take my place. The government would get its conspirator, while I got away."

I was a certified chump. "How I got to Santa Fe

didn't matter; that I did, did," I realized too late. "Agent Brand and Red-Bull were tailing you all over town. So you sobbed me a story and hoped I'd panic and take them out, leaving you scot-free. But why aren't you out of the country yet, Pixy?"

Pixy sighed, "I couldn't get the goods."

"What?"

"Like a lot of whizzes, Pfannenstiel has the brains, but not the ability, to make his ideas a reality. He needed artists to do mostly proof of concept drawings using this stretchy metal material called sentient steel. I got the job. I asked where he came up with the steel and he told me about the molecular assembler.

"Obviously, the thing was worth millions. I tried to get the blueprints. But Pfannenstiel only wanted me to draw pictures of shinier and brighter buildings, bridges, cars – sentient steel improvements to existing stuff. I tried to convince Pfannenstiel of the goldmine he was sitting on. But he wouldn't buy it. Eventually, I became his gofer: grading papers and getting coffee. I got fed up. At 35, how much can you take!"

I had to interrupt. "I thought you were 27, Pixy?"

"It's a woman's prerogative to change her mind," Pixy replied.

"And the minds of those around her?"

"Whatever works: it's a state of mind I thought someone like you might appreciate, Sonny. So, I contacted the right people. But they wanted more than the enhancements I'd drawn. They wanted diagrams, but I couldn't get them. So, I scrounged around the lab and found the steel. I thought the assembler could make more, so gave the sample to the buyer. Somehow, it did the trick. They said they'd pay me a million...*if I gave them the doctor, too.*

"So, they get Pfannenstiel and sentient steel. But they're responsible for getting the specs and the location of the assembler. As a bonus, I'm throwing in our not-so-secret agent. If Pfannenstiel wouldn't give Bambi or me the scoop on the assembler, maybe she sucked it out of him. If so, they can get the formula from her, if he still won't talk. If he didn't tell her, at least they'll have her to pump for her agency's scope and methods."

"Sounds like you have your bases covered," I responded to Pixy's plan. "But I didn't notice my name in the transaction."

Pixy threw her head back and began to laugh. "Well, Sonny, bullets are expensive and few. I can't afford to waste one, not even on you.

"You know, you're really not a bad kind of guy. The only questions you asked when we first hooked up were about how and when you were going to get paid. Unlike Bambi, you didn't get greedy: you took what I offered and were on your way. If that bitch fed hadn't stolen your car, you would have done your job. So, now that I'm a millionaire, I guess I can afford to give you another chance. So, why not share the risk and join me?"

"It's tempting," I said. "But…"

Pixy picked up on my concern and urged me not to be a fool. But I had to ask, "What's the risk worth? And what will my reward be where we're going?"

"It's worth more than another penny-ante case and it will buy you a longer lease on life. How's that?" Pixy asked.

I mulled over the word 'life.' "*A lease on life*, you say? I think it'll be life in prison, Pixy. The feds will deploy every agent, soldier, and sailor they've got. Hell, they'll even re-instate the draft to stop you from stealing the steel.

"You have brains, Pixy. But you should have used them to think this thing through. You didn't; so now, how's your brawn?"

Pixy jaw shifted to a smirk, and she slowly nodded her head. It was a nod of acceptance of my defiance. "You tell me, Sonny," she suggested.

That didn't sound good. What sounded worse was when Pixy snapped her fingers and, like trained Rottweilers, her supporting cast of bad actors moved into action. I dubbed the so-far nameless pair "Hans and Franz," borrowing the names from that old *Saturday Night Live* skit that spoofed the brawn-over-brains mindset of the weightlifting culture.

The floor seemed to shake when Hans – the taller blond – drew near. I think that's why I couldn't balance myself to throw a decent punch at him. Then again, my legs and arms quivered from fear and probably had more to do with it than tectonic shifting. Either way, I missed my shot, but Hans didn't. He ducked mine and took his: a solid uppercut that burrowed into my belly.

The Skyview booze and the PU pizza and pop poured out of me like I was a popped piñata. And I followed the putrid stream to the floor, where my knees hit and I rolled sideways. That was one way to lose all those calories. Except for the awful, immediate pain it caused. And that it left me crumpled and gasping – begging – for air.

Hans growled, "How is that for starters?"

"Not bad," I wheezed. Still clutching my stomach, I got as far up as to a knee. Then, the throbbing pain in my gut got the best of me, and I grumbled, "For a while, I thought you bastards were just props."

A smart mouth can be a handy tool in my trade, *if* you know when to use it. But I didn't. And now, it was going to get me screwed and drilled again. Because no sooner than I caught my breath did Franz – the shorter, bald bad actor – step up and take it away. He delivered what felt like a wrecking ball to my demolition, with a wicked, back-handed whack across my face that leveled me.

His punch line delivered more devastation – this time, to my ears. "Props on your busted chops, pops!" Franz snorted.

This time, it took me a lot longer to right the ship. When I fully came to, my blazer was gone – used to mop up the mess, as it was draped over my vomit. But I noticed something more important: Hans and Franz were carrying someone in on a stretcher. After the pasting they put on me, I thought they were carrying me. That I was having one of those out-of-body experiences: where you somehow step outside your skin and see your dead or dying body. Instead, the person Hans and Franz carried was Pfannenstiel. They set him down and left.

A door creaked open and slammed shut somewhere in the warehouse. Then a rolling sound edged closer into earshot until a big silver and black steamer trunk filled my view. When Franz unfastened the straps and buckles, I saw inside. A breathing apparatus fitted into the trunk's padded lining meant the chest was reserved for treasure – specifically, Dr. Pfannenstiel's wealth of knowledge.

Bevel spoke for the first time in a while. "You're smuggling the doctor out...in *that*?" she wanted to know. Then Bevel broke into laughter.

Again, Pixy wasn't fazed. "Go ahead: laugh, while you can. Because life won't be so funny for you much longer," she warned Bevel. "Harlan Red-Bull was a traitor. So, we fed him a lie: a lie that you both fell for. You flocked all your forces at the airports and based them near the border. But what did you pour into thousands of miles of shoreline?"

"So you're sneaking him out by ship – slick, Ms. Sage," Bevel said, sounding impressed at first. But then I watched her eyes narrow into a piercing stare that she shot straight for Pixy. Then the female fed growled a guarantee: "A ship is fitting transportation because one way or the other, you're going up the river for this!"

Pixy laughed at Bevel. "I doubt that very much," she remarked. "Your backup is chasing the Stealth and you're a pathetic, unarmed mess. So who's going to arrest me? A graveyard shift of low-paid dock workers and a security staff armed with pepper spray! They're lazy-asses when it comes to inspecting exports. But if they decide to be diligent, stuffing their pockets with big bills should slow them down. If not, bullets will."

Catfights fascinated me: how females change from cute little cubs to ripping, tearing lionesses. And Bevel's and Pixy's barbs were building into a doozy of a duel. But my attention shifted to the steamer trunk, in particular its breathing equipment.

There were two yellow canisters about an arm's length long (both probably full of oxygen) that were fitted with dials, pressure gauges and nozzles on top. Strapped on the side of the trunk was a breathing mask. An all-around typical setup...except. Except that the breathing mask wasn't hooked to the nozzle yet. That gave me an idea.

CHAPTER SIXTEEN

Bomb Voyage

I leaned Bevel's way and pretended to whisper in her ear. Pixy saw us and quickly yelled something to Hans and Franz in a foreign language. They responded by separating Bevel and me – exactly the reaction I wanted.

Hans grabbed the female fed and moved her nearer to Pixy. Pixy then shoved Bevel to the floor and pointed her pistol at her head. I was dragged over to the trunk, and callously reacquainted with the floor. I tried to move, but bumped into what felt like a pole. It turned out to be Franz's leg: he was standing guard over me, waiting to pounce with Pixy's permission.

Meanwhile, Pixy and Hans were ready to move Pfannenstiel. Both took one end of the stretcher and prepared to lift. Suddenly, Pixy was upended by a leg whip (delivered courtesy of Bevel Brand). Like the well-trained dog he was, Franz left me to rush to the aid of his fallen mistress. As for falls, it seemed all the breaks were descending my way: I was alone with the trunk!

Even with Pixy down, Bevel was outnumbered and overpowered by Hans and Franz. But she fearlessly kicked and clawed against their strength. Under commotion's cover, I carefully turned a little toward the trunk. Keeping an eye out for the possibility of Franz's sudden return, I slipped my hand inside and felt for the nozzle. Only the smooth, cool feel of a small piece of protruding steel confirmed I'd found it.

I turned the nozzle fast. Unable to see which direction I'd turned, only a faint hiss told me I succeeded in activating one of the oxygen tanks. I then quickly returned to my spot on the floor.

"I'm all right!" I heard Pixy tell Hans and Franz, as she shooed them away from helping her up.

Hans and Franz both managed to bust the bucking Bevel Brand and force her to her knees. It was the perfect level for Pixy to paste a nasty bitch-slap across Bevel's face. The female fed wilted, but I was so glad for her intuition. Bevel had read my mind about the trunk and the oxygen tanks. She caused the distraction, and took one wicked shot for the team.

Hans and Franz proceeded to lift the stretcher and Pfannenstiel. They got it as far as the trunk. But when I struggled to a knee, Hans and Franz sensed a confrontation coming on. They stopped short of packing up Pfannenstiel, clenched their fists on instinct instead, and moved toward me, looking for a fight. Pixy moved between them, blocking their advance by spreading her arms. Hans and Franz stopped and moved back. Pixy advised me not to be a hero, too.

"Are you kidding?" I replied. "I'm no match for your brawn, Pixy."

Pixy's ego seemed to swell at the sound of my submission. "So, you found it hard to beat after all, Sonny?"

"Absolutely, Ms. Sage," I said. "So unbeatable that it convinced me that I made a mistake in not taking you up on your offer to enlist. Is it still too late to join you guys?"

"I'm afraid so," Pixy said. "The one thing a woman hates most is being played for a fool. You've insulted my intelligence for the last time, Sonny."

"Well," I sighed, "before I die, don't I get a last request?"

"What is it?" Pixy impatiently snarled. I asked her for a cigarette. But Pixy fed me my old line. "They take seven minutes off your life with each puff." she mocked.

"*Perfect.* I'll only have to endure three minutes

of pain when you turn Hans and Franz over there loose on me," I replied.

Pixy burst into rowdy laughter. She told me to get up slowly. I wobbled up and limped over to her. That put me a little further from the trunk, but not too far for my plan to work. The only thing worrying me was how much oxygen was left in the one tank I was able to turn on.

Pixy reached into the breast pocket of her blouse and took out her cigarettes. She picked one out, parked it between her lips, and drew a lighter from her skirt pocket. Then out of the blue, Pixy grabbed me by my tie and yanked me down on my knees. Petite Pixy towered over me, grasping me by the tie. I felt like a dog on a leash.

Pixy loosened her grip and finally flicked the lighter. The cigarette lit up. Pixy took a long drag. She bent over and looked me in the eye. I finally got a smoke – a jet of smoke, I mean, from Pixy's mouth into my face. I gagged, much to the delight of Hans and Franz, who yakked it up behind me. *"There!"* Pixy shouted.

That wouldn't do; I had to get *my* hands on the cigarette! So I tried tapping into Pixy's pity. Most women have at least a trickle left, even after being done dirty. Though that trickle of mercy usually takes a few days to distill. "Come on, Pixy," I pleaded. "I'm beat: you're the best. What else can I say? Come on, one puff, please?"

Pixy grabbed me by my tie again and yanked me into her space, so close that we almost collided face to face. She removed the cigarette from her lips and gently placed it between mine. *At last!*

After that, Pixy let go of me, stepped back, and said, "So long, Sonny." She snapped her fingers, and I knew what that meant: I was dead meat – fit only to be served up to Hans and Franz.

But I grinned and took a puff. "*Bomb voyage* to you, too," I told Pixy.

As Hans and Franz closed in for the kill, I bravely blew a taunting stream of smoke at them. Then, I took the cigarette from my mouth, whirled around, and threw it at the trunk. I ducked and...*BOOYAH!*

I heard Hans and Franz scream and felt an intense wave of heat and debris steamroll me. When I determined it was safe, I raised my head from between my knees and looked around.

It was dim. The intense interrogation lamp was vaporized by the blast. A flickering amber arc from a couple low-watt lights lit the storeroom. The explosion had reduced the trunk to nothing more than a gleaming pile of red rubble. And behind it Hans and Franz lay motionless. On the other side of them was Bevel, her body spread-eagle over Pfannenstiel to protect him from the blast. Slowly, she rose to survey the damage.

My ears rang relentlessly and my back ached and felt wet (which meant I was bleeding and probably burned). But my adrenaline boosted me off my butt and back into action. Carefully, I moved toward Hans and Franz. I hoped they were dead, but found they weren't. I frisked them for weapons and was happily reunited with my trusty .357 and Salvador Khan's .32. But I'd need more artillery to keep Hans and Franz down once they came to. So, I added their guns (couple of .45 automatics) to my arsenal.

Suddenly, Bevel shouted, *"Sage!"*

Damn! I cursed myself. I'd forgotten about Pixy!

CHAPTER SEVENTEEN

Shifts in the Night

I frantically searched the room for Pixy Sage. All I saw were crates, boxes, and…there, against the far wall, was a large hole. The tear was too far to have been torn out by the explosion, but far enough to have been punched out by a panicked Pixy.

Bevel was already at the hole in the wall. I tried to follow, but my injured back flared up and put me down for a minute. By the time I regrouped, I saw Bevel balanced on the rim. Then she disappeared and I heard her scream.

I pocketed the .32 and the .357, shoved one of my two new .45s into my waistband, and readied the other .45 in my hand. I hurried for the far wall, but suddenly stumbled over something. It turned out to be Bevel Brand's discarded pumps. That woman was determined to keep me off the case one way or another. This time, it was by leaving her shoes for me to trip over!

At last, I got to the hole. I discovered it had been gouged out by a shotgun blast. And a gust of briny, biting air piped through. I bent over for a look outside when my injured back flared up and stopped me. I struggled to a recovery and craned my neck through the breezy breach.

Outside were wharfs and docks – City Harbor. But sloshing and thrashing sidetracked further scrutiny of my surroundings. When I looked down – five or six feet down – I saw Bevel Brand swimming like a champion: her long arms and legs purposefully propelling her away. Before I could see where she headed, rumbling caught my attention.

I searched for the source and picked out a hunched whitish object along the far pier. It betrayed human movements: a back bent and arms engaged in desperate back-and-forth jerks. Then I heard the rumble again, but this time it evened out into a buzz – like an engine starting up. The hunched, whitish posture straightened, and the light from the overhead dock lights revealed what looked like Pixy Sage. She had started a motorboat and her getaway.

I looked feverishly for Bevel, but this time couldn't see her. I hoped she had seen Pixy and was swimming for her. But I couldn't yell without alerting Pixy. There was only one way to stop Pixy: that was to shoot her.

I'd never killed anyone, just wounded a few fleeing hoodlums with shots in the leg or arm. And truthfully, the last time I'd seriously drawn a gun was three years ago. All the shooting I'd done since was at target ranges – to keep in shape. But now, I had to collect the courage to kill.

Pixy looked to be 80 yards away – just short of the length of a football field. Despite what you typically see in movies, when guys shoot and hit at almost any distance, most handguns have an effective range of less than 50 yards. To hit a far-away target, you have to set the gun's sights and then factor altitude, air temperature, and wind speed into the bullet's trajectory when aiming.

I was more familiar with revolver sights than automatics. My .357's fixed barrel sights would let me line up a more accurate shot: one that would get close to Pixy – maybe even hit her, if it was lucky. But firing the company gun off duty would get me fired. And Salvador Khan's .32 didn't have enough energy capacity in its small cartridge to do the trick. So, I fiddled with the formidable .45 automatic's sights and when finished, steadied myself into a firing position through the hole.

I took as accurate aim as my aching back and my gun would let me. I got off two rounds: one hit the water a good five feet from the boat. The other must have zoomed way off course. But both shots startled Pixy enough that she stopped trying to start the boat and ducked for cover. *Perfect!* I thought. That was until I heard another sound in the distance.

The sound was a faint buzz that became louder and more distinct as it approached. Shortly, it became apparent that it was another boat, but not the kind with the outboard motor Pixy struggled to start. And when I saw Pixy stand and wave her arms anxiously I gasped "oh shit!" because it looked like her pals were coming to the rescue.

Again, I looked for Bevel but saw no one. It looked like I was alone and left with the same solution as before: to try and take out my former client. Without Pixy's directions, I thought, it would take her fellow travelers awhile to search the shore for Pfannenstiel. That could buy me enough time to maybe escape.

I rummaged through the shack's crates and boxes and found some planks. The thickest, longest one was also the roughest one. But I took it and balanced it halfway though the hole. Like a surfer paddling out to catch a wave, I lay level on the board and wiggled through the hole. If one of my last two shots got within five feet of Pixy before, the stretch from the plank might give me the extra length to hit her. I got as far as my balance would let me and again, steadied my .45. But something stopped me from firing.

It was a familiar sound: a woman's scream. Only this time, it was Pixy's. I saw her lose her balance in the motorboat and plunge into the water. I waited to shoot at her once she emerged. Pixy bobbed up, but was flailing – like something had hold of her. I made out some arms and then a head that weren't of a sea monster, but of something more deadly: a female fed scorned. *Bevel Brand!* She and Pixy were finally locked in a catfight. Or more appropriate, a *catfish* fight. I'd never seen two women water wrestle. And it turned out that I wouldn't enjoy the event because, again, I was distracted.

One, then two, and finally three shiny water-crafts (with their motors roaring and knifepoint bows plowing through the green-and-gray soup) closed in on the women.

I cried *"Bevel!"* but the engines drowned me out. And I was in no condition to dive in and swim to Bevel's aid. Besides, I couldn't leave Pfannenstiel alone; I feared Hans and Franz would come to.

That's when I decided to wait until Pixy's buyers came ashore. Before firing on them, I'd take out Hans and Franz. And to keep sentient steel from falling into enemy hands, I'd whack Pfannenstiel next. Then, I'd set in on popping as many of Pixy's pals as I could, saving a final bullet for myself. So I prepared to slide back inside and search for a window to shoot from. The plan seemed sure-fire, straight from every action flick where the hero's back's to the wall.

Suddenly, brilliant searchlights set the waters

ablaze in blue. And one of the vivid rays swung around and washed over the warehouse. My patchwork sniper's perch was quickly exposed! Carefully, I wiggled my body back inside. I prayed Pixy's pals didn't have torpedoes or rocket-propelled grenades. If they did, they wouldn't have to go ashore, but could blow me to bits from their boats. My plan seemed dead in the water.

To hell with it! I thought. I took a deep breath and worked my way back through the hole. I was ready for a heroic last stand when the wail of sirens stopped me from firing. *It was the cavalry:* those super horse-powered watercrafts I worried over actually belonged to the harbor cops, the Coast Guard, the Navy – or maybe all three!

It was another of many shifts in the night – one more reversal of fortune. It looked like my ship had come in, and Pixy's was sinking. I smiled, wormed my way back through the hole, and pulled in safely.

My upper body was damp from the salty mist sprayed by the water war. All of a sudden, I couldn't feel my legs. Steadiness abruptly abandoned me, and I sensed I was sinking. The last thing solid I felt was the floor against my head.

I don't know how long I was out, but the sound of distant shouting woke me. I crawled to the hole and looked out. One watercraft was docked, its crew picking up Pixy. But I didn't see Bevel Brand on their boat. The other watercrafts pulled alongshore.

Black waves of Kevlar-covered, machinegun-toting commandoes spilled out, and it wasn't long before the tin warehouse rattled from the rising force of double-timing jackboots. But it was a calming kind of force – the kind of rumble that's a sign of much-needed rain arriving during a scorching summer day.

I fought to my feet and panned around the room. Hans and Franz were wiggling to life. And Pfannenstiel…was gone! *What!* I wasn't out long enough for someone else to have captured him. But before I could search the warehouse, crates and boxes burst from what was a barricaded entrance.

The commandoes poured through like a tsunami. And their voices, louder and deadlier in force than the trunk explosion, swept me off my feet when they roared, "Drop you weapons and get on the ground, now – now!"

So once again, I ducked and covered and felt the heat roll over me.

CHAPTER EIGHTEEN

As Clear as Mud

Well before the dawn's early light, the docks were quickly draped with the old red, white, and blue: the fire department, the ambulance, and the feds, I mean.

I saw the feds haul Hans and Franz away in chains and, with no Bevel Brand in sight, they got me, too. I tried to explain to them what had happened. It didn't work. And when I got to the part about blowing up the steamer trunk, the fire captain jumped on my already smarting back and laid into me for bomb-bursting in err.

I got an ambulance ride to the hospital to tend to my wounds (with two stern-faced federal marshals in tow). It turned out that I had several minor cuts and a deep bruise on my face. But amazingly, there were no broken bones from the stomach punch. The damage to my back from the trunk explosion turned out to be nothing more than deep abrasions that weren't severe. The nurse even found me a new shirt to replace my ragged one. *What luck!* Until I realized it didn't match my tie. So after a couple of hours, I was checked out, stitched up, salved, bandaged, and cleared.

No sooner than the doctor left did the two federal minders return to ship me out.

The marshals drove me to one of the many shiny, tidy, multimillion-dollar government tin cans downtown for what I was sure was booking. But I didn't see any outside label distinguishing what brand of alphabet soup snoop group was in the facility.

Once we cleared the routine, upper-level security checkpoints, the marshals and I stepped onto an elevator. It didn't take long to reach what I guessed was the dungeon. The marshals then escorted me to a white-padded interrogation room. They told me to sit and wait. I did, and the marshals left.

There I sat, idly waiting. It was the first cool and quiet safety I'd had all night, so I wasn't complaining. Besides, I had company: a couple of wall-mounted TV cameras and a two-way mirror opposite the table where I sat.

The TV cameras were comforting. A year ago, electronic recording of all custodial interrogations became law nationally. So things couldn't get out of hand, like in the old days (when interrogators often broke rules to break suspects). And I kept thinking Bevel Brand was behind the two-way mirror: telling the brass about my heroics and sadistically making me sweat before she would self-assuredly saunter in to save me.

The shock wave from the exploding trunk cracked my watch, so I had no way of knowing how long I sat in the interrogation room. It felt like an hour passed before the heavy door opened. But Bevel didn't open it or walk through.

Instead, two well-built white guys – anywhere from thirty-five to fifty in age – marched in. Their square jaws were clenched, brows angrily knit, and off-the-rack shirt sleeves rolled, revealing strong forearms. The only thing distinguishing the boys was their toys: the one with a Glock 9mm said, "I'm Bramble"; the one with a classic .38 simply said, "Thorne." That was as polite as they got.

Bramble fired first. "You're in deep," he said, leaning over the table toward me.

I nodded and remarked dryly, "Yeah: the basement of a federal facility."

"No, I mean aiding and abetting Commies!" Bramble made his comment clear.

"I think you mean *opportunists*," I smugly struck back.

"Opportunists come in all colors, smart ass!" Bramble blasted me: "Red, white…and in your case, black and blue."

Then Thorne pulled up a chair, turned it backwards, and sat beside me. He was playing the good cop to Bramble's bad. "You're in with a cruel crowd – internationally wanted types. Of course, you know that, being you're partners. So, why not fill us in on more of what they did tonight?" he weighed in.

"If they're wanted, do I get the reward money for turning on them?"

"*Ha, ha,*" Bramble snorted. "You know, we can hold your ass for a long time."

"Am I a suspect?" I asked. Neither interrogator answered. So I took it I was a material witness, which meant they would have to fish or cut bait quickly. But how long was "quick"?

If Pixy's pals posed an international threat, a judge would buy my interrogators' charge and approve my arrest or indefinite detention. So I backed off some. "Okay," I calmly replied. "For the umpteenth time tonight, *they* kidnapped a college prof, a federal agent, and me. They planned to kill me and smuggle the prof and the agent out."

"What a cover story," Bramble sneered. "They did it, not me – so imaginative!"

"Come on, pal: level with us," Thorne asked.

"I am a private investigator – check it out! And the only thing I'm guilty of is not closely checking out my client, who turned out to be one of the kidnappers."

"Sure, sure," Bramble said. "Looks like you're

gonna need one of those Left-loving civil liberties lawyers."

They weren't buying it. So I braced myself and said, "Okay, the truth. If this is cut-rate cop cinema, you two are putting on Emmy-winning performances."

That finally struck a nerve. Bramble growled, "Why you...," and dived across the table for me. Thorne restrained him and the interrogation room door banged open.

An official-looking Asian man in a blue suit and striped tie jumped in. "Get a hold of yourself!" he barked at Bramble.

"Sorry, chief," Bramble began to say, "but..."

"Cut him loose," the Asian man ordered his men.

"*What?*" Bramble and Thorne gasped together.

"You heard me," the Asian man said. "If you'll follow me, Mr. Busco, I'll show you the way out." I gladly obeyed. After we cleared the interrogation room, the man called "chief" officially introduced himself as Quo, Chief of Weapons and Narcotics Section. He said my story checked out. "Sorry it took so long to verify," Quo apologized.

"No problem," I said. "It probably took awhile to debrief Agent Brand. She was busy arresting Pixy."

"Our men, in tandem with units of the harbor police and a special Coast Guard detachment, apprehended Pixy Sage," Quo replied.

"Okay. But Agent Brand told you I was inno-cent, right?" I asked.

Quo's faced twisted. *"Agent Brand?"* he replied.

"Yeah, Special Federal Agent Bevel Brand. I tried to tell your guys earlier that I helped her save Dr. Ferris Pfannenstiel of Premier Studies University."

Like his men, Quo refuted my claim. "There was no such agent or doctor at the scene. What's more, there isn't an Agent Brand under my command," he said. "Now, Mr. Busco, the local PD verified that their detectives questioned you regarding the murder of a college coed. You're pretty much cleared from being the shooter. Early ballistics report made the murder weapon out to be a sniper rifle. That corroborates your claim of escorting the coed to the library."

"Thanks," I told Quo. "That's a big load off my mind!"

"Additionally, the PD responded earlier tonight to shots fired outside the Atlas Club. They picked up some parking lot video of what turned out to be the carjacking of a Dodge Stealth. They traced it to a Cruise Again auto repair shop, and the owner said he rented it to you for your case. So, an APB was put out on your car. It was stopped for speeding and the driver arrested for possession of a stolen vehicle. The locals impounded the car and found a stolen government tracking device and $1,250 in counterfeit bills."

"What about my client, Pixy Sage?" I asked.

"You were right back there: you should pick your future clients more carefully, Mr. Busco," Quo advised. "It turns out Sage's hoodlum buddies are internationally wanted. The two you bested in the warehouse still won't crack: they're pros. But the scared kid driving the stolen Stealth sang the story."

"What story: That he was a decoy, while Sage kidnapped her college professor?"

Quo laughed, "Mister Busco, you termed my agents' interrogation technique an 'Emmy-worthy performance.' But frankly, your insistence that there is some professor and mystery agent we're hiding from you is Oscar-caliber creative."

"Bramble and Thorne won't like that," I replied.

"*What?*"

"That they're only TV talent, while a civilian like me has silver screen stuff."

Quo's smile was thinner this time. But he told me a little more. "Look, all I can say is that the local cops verified that your car was stolen. And the thief's story led them to believe you were kidnapped for stumbling onto Ms. Sage's operation."

"*What* operation, sir?"

"Drugs and guns," Quo said.

Drugs and guns? What a lie! I struggled to keep from losing it.

"Sage's cronies are expert traffickers. They're wanted for drugs and arms dealing as well as for and bribery and assassination. The kid who stole the Stealth said Sage and her partners were planning to pick up a shipment of smack coming in. The cops called us, we alerted our people at several locations, and got there just in time to rescue you. You were instrumental in uncovering smugglers and contraband, Mr. Busco."

I had to try and recover something out of this. So I played my usual angle. "So what's my part in all this worth, chief?"

"Well, the fewer people who know about this, the better. It's for your safety," was the value Quo placed on my heroics. "How would it look with you on TV receiving an award when Sage and her gang think you've been arrested and jailed? You getting paid off would make them only want payback. I know that isn't much, but rest assured that we owe you a great deal that we can never fully repay, Mr. Busco."

"Well, there's always the installment plan, chief," I suggested. This time, Quo gave me a pat on the shoulder, but no smile. "If you could just take care of my hospital bill and square away any PD ideas that I conspired to kill that coed, I'd call it even."

"We'll look into that, Mr. Busco," Quo replied, with a smile. "Oh, you can reclaim your rental car and possessions at Police Station 44. Do you need a ride there?"

I declined the offer, and Quo shook my hand. Then I was ushered out of the depths of the government building. Once topside, I looked outside and noticed the night began to fade into dawn. And my understanding of the past night's events was just as murky as the milky morning sky. It was all as clear as mud, as they'd say back home.

CHAPTER NINETEEN

Curiosity Rekindled

The bus ride to Police Station 44 to pick up my impounded car was long but thankfully without incident. Not only did it give me a chance to rest my sore body, it gave me time to think about last night, and to try to put the puzzling picture together.

I knew what happened didn't involve drugs or guns, other than the drugs Pixy pumped into Pfannenstiel and the guns her pals repeatedly put in my face. I figured Bramble and Thorne's bungled interrogation was all part of the whole show Quo cooked-up. It was probably also a scare tactic: a warning of what kind of federal harassment I could expect *if* I didn't play ball and keep my mouth shut. I was a hero, but an expendable one.

The bus dropped me off at the police station around 8 AM, and I picked up the Stealth and most of my belongings. The only thing the cops kept was the $1,250 in funny money that Pixy paid me up front. That kept me from having the feds hound me for another crime I didn't commit – counterfeiting.

At about 10:30 AM, I returned the Stealth to Hub Wheeler. He was happy to get it back in one piece, and I was happy to have the familiar feel of my Olds. I told Hub that nothing much became of the case other than it turned out my client bilked me and that I turned her over to the cops for fraud.

Hub's ever-suspicious mind wouldn't let him fully buy that (since the cops called Cruise Again for the scoop on the stolen Stealth). Hub thought I was in on something big, but was told not to blab – *true*.

I left Cruise Again and about ten minutes later, pulled up to a supermarket payphone. I took some change from the ashtray and punched up Premier Studies University. I asked for Dr. Pfannenstiel's office. Since it was during business hours, I figured I could talk to the doc directly (without the hassle of smug assistants as before). But his office told me he was on sabbatical. I thanked the secretary, laughed at the lie she'd been told, and hung up.

It was a little after noon when I stopped by Estado Dorado's Wheel and Deal, where I gave Salvador Khan his .32 back. He was happy to get his gun; happier that I used my head and kept from killing the beautiful burglar.

I didn't get home until close to 2:30 PM. The first

thing I did after entering my apartment was head straight to my bathroom. I popped some Tylenol for the aches and pains and then went into the living room and crashed on the couch. But I didn't get the sleep I needed. Instead, I tossed and turned and thought about what had happened again. After an hour or so, it boiled down to two things: that I was still in debt, but not dead. In the end, I was no worse off than before I'd taken the case.

My internal clock awakened me for the news at a quarter 'til five. I felt a little better and clicked on the TV. To my surprise, I saw the case of my life lead the local news. Quo suggested keeping it all under wraps. But the bottle-blond Ken and Barbie anchors and their bold reporters broadcast it to the whole city!

As I watched, I realized they bought the whole drugs and gun bust cover story after all! Because the footage was of the harbor patrol racing in their speedboats to confiscate the tons of smack in the shack that Quo told me I'd helped stop from entering the country. But the bad guys they showed being herded into custody weren't the bad guys I helped nab. No innocent-looking Pixy or Hans's or Franz's faces. In their place were a band of medium- to dark-skinned Mexicans and Caribbean men, with hands above their heads or behind their backs. *The usual suspects,* I thought.

With my curiosity in the case rekindled, I

flipped from channel to channel to see if there was any change in coverage. Sadly there wasn't. I got to El canal de noticias Espanola (the Spanish News Channel). But the only difference in their coverage was that a slightly tanned, dark-haired Ken and Barbie pair chronicled the case in Spanish.

Worn-out, I tuned out and turned off the TV. I headed for the kitchen, where I fixed myself a double-decker sandwich full of all the cold cuts left in the fridge. Then, I grabbed a bottle of Coca-Cola and headed back to the living room. After I ate, I left my desk for the couch. Full of food, I finally dozed off.

It didn't seem long before the alarm clock rattled me awake. It was dark outside: time for guard duty. I stretched the kinks out of my arms, got dressed, armed, and off to work. But I wasn't as laid-back as usual. I felt like a real security guard, not just rental property.

I was wide-eyed and jittery. I suspected every customer in the store of being assassins sent by Hans's and Franz's organization to kill me for ruining their shot at securing sentient steel. Babies' bulging diapers bulged because they concealed grenades. Old ladies only acted feeble – in the way Pixy tricked me with her naïve schoolgirl getup – in order to take advantage of my backwoods, Midwestern warmth and then whack me.

In a weird way, though, that night was the first

time I actually did my job as a guard correctly. I mean, I made people think twice about shoplifting or committing robbery. My sturdy-stare-and-thumbs-hooking-my-gun-belt, quick-draw pose put more fear into the shoppers than before.

When the store closed, my nerves didn't ease any. I had to walk to the parking lot to the company truck. And I remembered immediately what happened the last time I walked into a parking lot. It was at the Atlas Club. So this time, I took no chances and pulled out my .357 in advance. I got to the truck and gave it a careful looking over: in the flatbed, beneath the truck, and behind and under the seats in the cab. This time, there was no trouble. I got in, started up, and tore out of the lot on route to my last assignment.

It was five 'til nine when I pulled into my last business. They were closed, and I was simply to sit in the truck and watch for anything suspicious until I was relieved by the next guard shift. This time, there weren't dozens of people parading around me every minute. So my mind relaxed and drifted back to normal thoughts...like the fact that I'd missed the ball game. I turned on the radio and surfed the dial for the post-game highlights show when something happened.

Instead of the wrap-up show, I coasted into the tail-end of a syndicated AM talk show. The host said he'd be back with some special guests. Then I caught the show's name: *Cloak and Dagger Chatter.* I'd never listened to it before because it was Hub Wheeler's favorite program.

The wacko show is a mega-watt, mega-hit spotlight that exposes secrets, from sea to shining sea. It's the source for much of Hub's spouting about what the system's doing to us behind the scenes. I used to blow it off as no more than a nightly remake of the old Orson Welles radio gloom and doom dramas. But now I had a deep, dark, and gnawing secret and wanted to hear how others dealt with theirs.

At 9 PM, the host (who broadcasts from the depths of a decommissioned, renovated Minuteman missile silo somewhere in the Dakotas) introduced his promised guests. The anonymous pair (dubbed "Agents X" by the host) claimed they were once government agents who now had, of course, a secret to spill. What they had to say, though, was mostly bull.

Mainly, they claimed they were assigned by the aeronautics research wing of government to dress up like aliens and to abduct anyone who got too close to secret federal space facilities. One of the "Agents X" mentioned the word "disinformation" during the interview. And all of a sudden, I sat up and took notice.

Through the course of the show, everything about sentient steel and that molecule making machine Bevel bothered herself about began to make sense. Things made so much sense that I didn't stick around for the next secret to be uncovered after the top-of-the-hour break.

Instead, I tuned into a sappy relationships show and just relaxed to the sound of ordinary conversation. And when I got home around 2 ᴀᴍ, I finally slept…like a baby.

CHAPTER TWENTY

Faking the Deal

A week passed and I felt ready to close the file on sentient steel. I concluded that as a private detective, my job was simply to collect information for a client or to protect a client. I did both. The difference was my real client in the steel deal was capitalism. And as funny as it sounds, it was put at risk by a man who played by its rules: by investing his time and money to build something to sell. But selling his miracle molecule-making machine would have crashed the free market because it could create everything anyone would need – except common sense. So, I helped the feds – a faction whose actions at times defy common sense – cover it up. As we used to say back in the day, *crazy!*

But I thought about my youth for a moment. About the Civil Rights Movement and Vietnam:

two of my generation's bloodiest, ultimate sacrifices for king and country. I was a few years too young to have participated in them, but fully reaped their rewards.

So, I chalked up the steel deal as *pro bono* work or community service – as me following JFK's call to "ask not what my country could do for me, but what I could do for my country." And different from those who went to Nam or who struggled for Civil Rights, I didn't lose life, limb, or sanity for doing my part. It just cost me my usual fee.

Weeks later, the events behind the steel deal surfaced. And about two months later, they officially wrapped up. But the official version was a shadow of what I know really happened.

It turned out that the whole sentient steel and molecular assembler stuff was swept under the rug. For one thing, prosecutors often like easy-to-prove, slam-dunk cases that don't involve complex, entangling webs of people, places, and things that take up valuable time and money investigating. Talk of a revolutionary alloy produced by a system of sentient micro robots was definitely too difficult to prove or even believe. And the feds wouldn't pursue treason charges because there would be Congressional hearings on the kind of the secrets Pixy tried to steal, thus exposing all that really happened.

So when the media got a hold of the steel deal, they set to work smearing it with a thick topping of scandal and sleaze. The public ate it up. And once full of delicious deception, hardly anyone cared about the meat and potatoes of it all – the truth.

Drug busts aren't the big news they once were. The TV and radio talk shows needed a show-stopper of a story. At first, they ran with the whole violence on campus thing. That Pixy conspired to kill Bambi so she could become club president. But that didn't get big ratings either. So, the media dug into Pfannenstiel's background (since he was the club sponsor). And that's when the whole thing became a sideshow.

Turns out Santa Fe was Pfannenstiel's hometown. Santa Fe was also home to a lot of what Haji Savante called "junk science" enterprises. A lot of fly-by-night, storefront colleges and companies that offered training and degrees in New Age nonsense stuff: astral projection, psychic research, alternative healing, and space alien investigation. In fact, a few hundred miles from Santa Fe, the whole UFO craze got started. Near Roswell, New Mexico, it's claimed, aliens crash-landed in 1947.

The tabloids ran with a "tip" that Pfannenstiel based his research on supposedly finding a piece of that crashed alien ship's metal in the desert outside Albuquerque, New Mexico. Once that broke, Pfannenstiel was labeled a "fringe science professor."

But ratings finally went through the roof when it broke that Pixy, Bambi, and Pfannenstiel were actually involved in a drugs and love triangle. And that Pixy, in a fit of jealous rage, conspired to kill Bambi. One rag's headline even read, "Bespectacled Batty Beast Slays Campus Beauty."

It was no coincidence that Pfannenstiel shortly resigned from PU, citing only that he felt responsible for not realizing "the undercurrents of the club and its members." And that his "pursuit of scientific truth blinded him to what the club was supposed to stand for: helping people by educating them of the benefits and dangers of technology."

I thought the media's reduction of Pfannenstiel's status to a quack and entangling Pixy in a love triangle helped Bevel's group tremendously. It was a way of making any would-be spies think twice about seriously pursuing tales of far-out technology.

As for Hans and Franz, both were extradited to Colombia – not Germany or Russia – to stand trial for everything from trafficking to bribery to assassination. And there was no mention of what happened to the kid who drove the Stealth and sang to the cops. That left Pixy Sage alone to weather the storm.

The local PD ballistics matched the .25 caliber bullet that killed Bambi to an AR-7 folding sniper rifle – a weapon light enough for a little lady like Pixy to possibly point and then pop the techno club president.

But the cops didn't have the weapon to dust for

Pixy's fingerprints. And with Hans and Franz extradited and Bevel and Pfannenstiel MIA, the only witness left was me. And though I had been kidnapped, a defense attorney would have a field day picking apart my credibility. There were parts of my past and my current debt to exploit. But biggest of all, I accepted Pixy's offer; though I did so without knowing her background or intentions.

Luckily, the cops drudged up Bambi's diaries (all written on hemp paper). They contained enough stuff about the bad blood between Pixy and her to charge Pixy with conspiracy to commit murder. But with the help of a high-priced attorney, Pixy could have beaten the conspiracy to commit murder rap. The diaries were circumstantial and composed by a pot-smoking, dope-dealing coed.

Pixy was also brought up on multiple drug trafficking charges and kidnapping. Those are ironclad felonies that even a law student could make stick. But in the end, Pixy skated with a plea bargain that got her a sweetheart 20 to life concurrent sentence (with parole consideration in 15). How did she pull that off? By offering up Satan on a silver platter? *Nah.* Without the Devil's deeds, where would D.A.'s be?

Instead, Pixy probably pulled every female desperation tactic from her skirt pocket. Every one Salvador Khan schooled me on. Pixy probably tried buying leniency by batting her eyelashes, shedding some tears, and saying she was duped into everything.

But since there was more to the steel deal than met the eye, members of Bevel Brand's band probably got to the D.A. and *advised* him to cut a deal. Or those same forces got to Pixy and *advised* her to play along with the drug story (as they did with me).

Or maybe Pixy read the tea leaves on her own. She could plead insanity, using the steel deal and all its entanglements as a defense. But given her smarts, and the circumstantial dirt between Bambi and her, it's doubtful a jury would buy it.

So, I took off my conspiracy cap and faced the reality that Pixy probably turned over information on Hans and Franz (or their organization) in exchange for a lighter sentence. She may have even sweetened the deal with dope on Bambi's pot-smoking pals at PU. Of course, ratting out drug dealers usually means you're trading your life for those fewer years in the pokey.

Some would say the drug charges better fit the techno-ethics club anyway. After all, the club's cuckoo credo of slow and steady progress when the world desperately needed radical changes for festering problems sounded like a lot of Purple Haze craze. And none of the top pecking order practiced what they preached. The convicted pot-smoking, dope-peddling president Bambi Wiles; Pixy; and Haji Savante, the Judas who deserted the divine

Dr. P for $50 –all were out for themselves, not the greater good.

In the end, we all faked the deal. The feds, the media, and I made sentient steel an urban legend: another crazy conspiracy theory for guys like Hub Wheeler to gnaw on.

CHAPTER TWENTY-ONE

The Old Ennui

My life finally returned to "the old ennui" from Cole Porter's "I Get a Kick out of You." That meant picking up a few marital infidelity cases – the hottest, most reliable job in the business. They're a sure bet. Just hire some hot bait (from a model, talent, or escort service) to sweet-talk suspects into acts of unfaithfulness, capture it all on audio and video, and present it to the suspicious spouse. *Easy.* But when you work alone, you barely break even after expenses. So, it's better to have several marital cases lined up.

I collected enough from a couple of open-and-shut cheater cases to finally pay off Gator Grimes. But no sooner than I got out of that ditch did I fall into another. I didn't have enough to pay the electric bill. Then the water and gas were shut off. But that wasn't too bad; I still had a roof over my head. I left for work a little after dawn and came home from work a little before dawn. I enjoyed little of my apartment, other than my pillow. But all that menial work was enough to keep the car and me running and the rent paid.

But early one June morning, the routine ran aground.

I got home after 5 AM and found the elevator broken. Nothing unusual about that. So, I slogged the stairs to my apartment. I found my door and my keys, but not necessarily in that order. I unlocked the door and plodded in. The gray dawn dappled the living room window's Venetian blinds and leaked across the faded carpet. That made it visible enough for me to walk a ways before having to turn on the lights.

It was also light enough in the living room for me to make out something covering my couch – a silhouette. *Dammit!* Was it one of Gator Grimes's guys with some loan shark logic that allowed him to shake me down for more dinero? No: It was worse. Something I forgot about from months ago must have finally come true: Hans's and Franz's friends found me!

I whipped my .357 from its holster, but was too late. The battery-powered end table lamp clicked on and I was struck point blank. But it wasn't by a bullet (though for awhile, I thought my uninvited guest would send one my way).

Instead, I was greeted by a shiny, black raincoat and long legs that slithered into sexy, sling-back heels. And the wearer greeted me in that arresting contralto, a voice that teetered on a purr or a growl. "Good morning," Bevel Brand breathed.

I lowered my revolver and borrowed Bevel's line. "Long time, no see," I said.

Then, she stole mine. "I think that's my line, stranger," Bevel replied.

"What kept you?"

"You know women: we tend to have a hang-up about looking just right."

"I thought it was for *the right guy*, not just any male chauvinist pig.'

Bevel didn't reply, except to grin.

"Well, it only took four months to powder your nose. But what a job you did."

I was a little more relieved that I wasn't entertaining an angel of death – or at least not entertaining one unaware. So, I holstered the gun and trudged past Bevel into the kitchenette. Once there, I took a jug of juice from the improvised fridge – an old beer cooler full of ice. I got two glasses from the cabinet and walked into the living room.

Bevel hadn't moved an inch. I asked if she wanted any orange juice. When my guest graciously declined, I flipped the cap and chugged from the jug. I went to my desk, plunked down in my swivel chair, and propped my big boots up on the desktop.

"Drinking from the jug and putting my feet up on the furniture would drive most chicks off, you know," I told Bevel.

"Sounds like you've had practice at that," was her still unmoved reaction.

"Practice?" I laughed. "I'm a pro. I'm also smart, reliable, funny, and daring. Everything women say they want in men, right? Except that I'm not rich." That's when my humor let up. "No money is what drives most chicks off."

"A lack of confidence drives most chicks off," Bevel asserted. Then, her tone lifted a little. "But lucky for you that I'm not *most* chicks."

"That's right," I groaned at the realization: "You're brassy Bevel Brand: tough, resourceful..., but just too damned attractive to be a good spy."

"Precisely why I'm not a spy, Mr. Busco; I catch them, instead," Bevel said.

"You're in counterintelligence, huh?" I replied indifferently.

More and more, the steel deal began to make sense. I remembered when the stuff came out about the notorious COINTELPRO (counterintelligence programs) of the '60s and '70s. How some fanatical feds snooped on Martin Luther King, Jr., and disrupted other political activist groups with paid infiltrators, half truths, and lies. It was shocking news to everyone…*but the black community*. Being one of the biggest targets of COINTELPRO, a lot of us knew about their tactics from the get-go.

Almost three generations later, I was listening to Bevel Brand legitimize the line of work. "Most people associate espionage with high glamour," she said. "Heroes and their sexy sidekicks in striking locations and armed with wonder gadgets to steal the secret plans and save the day with."

"Sounds like the whole sentient steel deal!" I laughed.

Bevel grunted, "That rarely happens, Mr. Busco. Intel work is mostly a lot of preparation: watching and waiting. It's like planting a seed: You wait for it to grow; you fight off a few pests; and, if everything goes right, you reap the wrong-doers in the end."

"It's a little like being a P.I.," I replied. "Only I dig up dirt, but don't drop seeds. And the fruits from my cases aren't as juicy as those under your jurisdiction."

"True," Bevel replied, "but believe it or not, most spies are like the common criminals you go after. They're personal failures who often lie and steal out of desperation – to give some meaning to their lives.

"I used to think spies' biggest motivation was some global political philosophy. Not so much. Instead, the fantasy of espionage being glamorous spurs most spies on today. It's a powerful incentive, but can be just as powerful a tool to catch them."

I grunted my agreement. *"Uh-huh,"* I said, between gulps of more juice. I wiped some of the spilled o.j. off the corner of my mouth with the sleeve of my windbreaker. That didn't bother Bevel either. "Well, tell Quo he doesn't have to worry. I'm sticking with the cover story of helping to bring down drug dealers, should anyone ever ask what I was doing on the dock of the bay.

"But tell Quo he could have spiced it up for the TV cameras by saying the guys we nabbed were narco-terrorists, instead of just your run-of-the-mill pot peddlers."

Bevel looked confused for the first time. *"Quo?"* she queried.

"That's probably not his real name," I replied.

"I'm not working for a 'Quo.'"

"Even if you're not working for his agency, the government's full of different agencies and agendas," I said. "I've heard your agency's agenda: to stop spies. But what's *your* agenda, Agent Brand? Why are you here in my apartment?"

Bevel tried an excuse on for size. *"To get out of the rain?"* she asked.

"It's partly the smog. It causes it to *look* like rain in the mornings – even all day, sometimes. But it rarely rains," I assured her.

"But I thought it *never* rains in..."

"The song starts out with *"seems* it never rains...," I corrected Bevel. "So, what's with the raincoat? What are you hiding underneath, or is that a secret?"

"Just my umbrella," Bevel said.

"What caliber?" I snorted. I took another swig of juice. "Well, Bev, don't worry: I'm not going to spill the beans. Not that anyone would believe me anyway. The official story is scholars collared and killed for drugs and sex. But Quo was right: Sentient steel, Pfannenstiel…all of it *was* a crock. I stepped into a pile of red herrings."

From the look on Bevel's face, my comments succeeded in stumping her for a second time. *"Red herrings?"* she asked. "Is your drink juiced with something other than pure oranges, Mr. Busco?"

I grinned and guaranteed Bevel that "trying to find out what the feds are up to will smash you a whole lot quicker than liquor!" Then, I got serious. "Red herrings," I began to clarify the term: "it means sentient steel was a front, an act, a put-on-for-show. Or, in a term you're probably more familiar with, it was disinformation."

That seemed to interest my guest. She uncoiled from her feline pose on my black vinyl couch and strolled over to my desk. Bevel then pushed the stacks of stuff off the desktop and sat on the edge. She crossed her long, shapely legs and swung them back and forth.

It was another of her charms. I think she was trying to hypnotize me with their brown sugary seduction. It was working, too, until the female fed offered, "A dime for your deductions, detective."

I sat up straight in my seat at the prospect of payment and blurted back, "I have a dozen or so deductions, and I need dough. Make it a dollar a deduction and you got a deal!"

"Still the comedian," Bevel laughed softly.

"So, is that all my deductions are worth: a laugh?"

"*Bring it, Mr. Busco,*" Bevel challenged me. "Let's see what you've got."

"If you're going to slang it, you should deep-six the dignified air. Let's go with Bev and Sonny, dig?"

Bevel paused for a moment, then smiled, and answered, "Solid...*Sonny.*"

So I eased back in my swivel chair, folded my hands peacefully on my lap, and finally laid out what would turn out to be a dissertation of a deduction.

CHAPTER TWENTY-TWO

The Steel Deal

"That bear you said you were loaded for – the big, bad one who threatened more than just campers – got me thinking," I said. "You know, we're supposed to be out of the Cold War wilderness, Bev. The eagle and the bear are buddies, right? But all I see is the same old game: bears and eagles chasing each other. Only now, it's to catch each others' red herrings. Yeah, the steel deal was one doozy of a disinformation operation.

"I bet better stuff than a miracle-making molecule machine exists, but is tucked away – maybe in Santa Fe? To distract foreign efforts to find it, you planted a Dr. Ferris Pfannenstiel and his revolutionary invention at a prestigious state university."

Bevel gasped, *"Planted?* Don't tell me you think Dr. Pfannenstiel's a phony."

"Not totally," I replied. "He's a scientist, with degrees up to his knees. But you hired him and gave him a phony invention as bait for uncovering the Russian spy network."

Bevel butted in with "Sonny, a lot of Pfannenstiel's studies were open to question. Why hire someone with so much baggage to work what you claim was such a sensitive secret operation?"

"His faults were just what the doctor ordered," I replied. "You don't always want someone squeaky-clean dishing disinformation. The other side usually prefers an approachable target: someone who is broke, depressed, or addicted – someone whose flaws they can take advantage of. By the same token, you want someone working the sting who, if caught or defects, you can easily disown by revealing his flaws.

"American and Russian intelligence had to have already confirmed Pfannenstiel's whole life's story – the good and the bad. All we needed was his legit nanotechnology research to bait the Russians. And the Russians, after taking the sentient steel bait, thought Pfannenstiel may have stumbled onto something useful, despite his past."

"But Sonny, you said the Russians are our allies," Bevel said.

"*Broke allies,*" I quickly demoted their status. "And allies still have their own problems and their own interests, Bev. They're not above stealing to solve them."

Bevel shrugged. "So, they have fallen on hard times," she remarked indifferently. "Reduced circumstances can make you spend more wisely and carefully, not steal."

"All they have is a dream: to get back their bite – the superpower status they lost. When you've had it all, sometimes, you will go for broke in hopes of regaining it fast."

"They have more than *a dream*, Sonny. They still have hundreds of nukes."

"It used to be thousands. But they couldn't maintain them anymore than they could their country, Bev. Nukes alone can't boost your economy; new inventions and technology can. That's why they risked so much going for the maker of sentient steel."

"But Sonny, you're making sentient steel sound like the real deal all along."

"It's real, but not the real McCoy. Some of the best lies have elements of truth to them. I think the steel was real, but something you found – a freak of nature. Like a meteorite or a fossil. But it's harmless, since it can't be reproduced."

"But a mere meteorite or fossil can't at all do what sentient steel does," Bevel argued. "You don't leave something that special lying around."

"You do if you have more special stuff in the wings. Like I said, Bev, there are better things than one piece of steel that we're trying to hide. After all, what good is one piece of this stuff? In such a small amount, what can you really do with it? Weave it into better bulletproof vest for the president, or beat it into a better bumper for his limo?

"Something like sentient steel really belongs in a museum, for customers to pay to see. But you don't want it seen by everyone. Just by a few. And those few are spies. So, it's excellent bait – a way to focus the spies on the steel, instead of the real deal.

"So, what's the harm in leaving it lying around, instead of risking leaving half-baked assembler plans that Russian scientists could quickly determine aren't up to specs? That's why Pixy couldn't get the blueprints: they didn't exist.

"Instead, Pixy found the supposedly sacred steel lying around in Pfannenstiel's lab. I think he left it there for her to lift; he knew her intention. So the Russians got it, studied it, and found they couldn't re-create it. That made them *think* the story about molecular assembler creating it was true and worth paying Pixy to pocket Pfannenstiel."

"A million bucks for a man, instead of the machine!" Bevel marveled.

"What if they got the machine and it was damaged? If their technicians can't figure out how to duplicate sentient steel, how likely is it they can fix the machine that created it? They would be back to square one: having something unique, but useless. They went for the inventor, so he could show them how to build and fix his invention."

"Also, you made it seem easier for them to get the man than the machine because of your cover story for Pfannenstiel: that of an independent, public college professor. An independent scientist is easier to approach than a watched-over government one."

Bevel laughed, "It sounds like you think we forced Premier Studies University to hire Pfannenstiel, regardless of their hiring policies? Do you know how many people go to that university – how many *educated* people? *If* you're right, Sonny, do you know how many of them we'd have to…?"

"Pay off or put down?" I cut-in.

"Ask to help," Bevel replied more delicately.

"Not many," I answered. "Educated doesn't mean informed, Bev. All you have to do is make sure *the right people* know what you're doing and why. And there are few of the right people to inform – usually, just the brass. You get them in your camp by giving them plenty of government goodies. Then they issue your orders for everyone to follow.

"I read that back in World War II, the Manhattan Project cost $2 billion and employed over 100,000 people. Did the secret about the atomic bomb get out? No, because only a few people at the top knew what was being built and why. It's the oldest trick in the business, Bev."

"They lacked 24/7 news coverage. That's why it didn't get out," Bevel quarreled.

"So we have more news? Are we any more

informed? With all our extra channels and coverage, everybody thinks the steel deal was about drugs, sex, and murder."

Bevel didn't seem to have an argument against that. She told me, "Go on, Sonny."

"I should have seen a scientist shell game when Pfannenstiel's t.a. told me the doctor was into "real science" and "modernization," while Pixy said he'd created a "revolutionary invention". Pfannenstiel walked a fine line: promoting real world technology to his students (so as to look legit to the faculty) and at the same time "junk science" to Pixy (in order to lure the Russians in).

"It also was a big help that Pixy was an art major. With limited technical expertise, she couldn't know if the machine she was drawing was real or fake. She didn't even know what she was looking for until the Russians hinted that what she had was worth kidnapping the inventor for. Pixy saw dollars, instead of sense.

"But I didn't catch on to the con until Pixy complained about not being able to pry the specs for the molecular assembler from the doctor. She couldn't get them because, as I've said, they didn't exist. So if Pixy and her pals resorted to torturing Pfannenstiel, all he would confess to was maybe finding the steel, but not knowing how it was created. Remember, one blemish on his record was he claimed to have found UFO wreckage.

"It was also handy to have the doctor laid out in plain sight: like a plum ready for picking. The mansion in Golden View Heights was another tip-off that there was more to this than met the eye. From outside, the mansion was glitzy; but inside, it was barely furnished. At first, I thought the mansion was a safe house.

"Then it hit me: the level of security didn't match the importance of the mission. Just one woefully armed and dressed woman who looked like she was interviewing for a job rather than doing the dangerous job of protecting what could be the next Einstein."

"*Ouch!*" Bevel cut in.

"Sorry," I laughed.

"Just the umbrella you think I'm concealing: it rubbed me the wrong way. That's what I get for dressing for rain when there is none. *Overdressing, again,*" Bevel muttered.

"Well, the whole setup was vulnerable, right down to the open sliding doors," I continued. "The mansion was more bait: to give the illusion of the wealth the steel could bring. Or maybe, the prosperity Pfannenstiel gained but couldn't keep up without more money. Money the Russians were willing to give in exchange for his invention. And you thought you'd hooked a spy taking the bait – me, by showing up at the mansion."

"The downtown taxi chase convinced you that

Pixy and I were partners from the get-go. But I was supposed to deliver sentient steel to Santa Fe, not show up and help kidnap Pfannenstiel. When Pixy found out the Stealth was in Golden View Heights, it told her something was wrong. Even before that, when I showed up on PU campus, Pixy knew something smelled. Speaking of Pixy, she used that techno-ethics club as a front."

"*A college club as part of your alleged counter-espionage operation?* This I'm very interested in hearing you explain, Sonny!" Bevel said.

"Okay," I replied, "criminals usually set up fronts: lawful activities that cover-up their illegal acts. PU's techno-ethics club was a perfect front. Pixy joined with the ulterior motive of using the club to break Pfannenstiel. She admitted to getting bubble-brained Bambi elected president so she could use her beauty to seduce the assembler secrets from him.

"But one club member, Haji Savante, was a problem. You were nervous of his plan to profit off new technologies with his newsletter. Maybe one of those new technologies was sentient steel. It might have ruined your COINTELPRO and opened your method of capturing spies to a wider audience – one that might include more developed countries than Russia. So, Pfannenstiel signed on. His money and mental power made Haji feel the club was legitimate after all and growing. Pfannenstiel got Haji to run for a lower club office to distract him from his newsletter. And Pixy was thrilled with Haji's satisfaction because she could control the club through Bambi's presidency. In the end, both sides used those poor kids as a front, hoping to use them to out the other's activities.

"Quo said Hans and Franz – Pixy's partners – were into, among other things, drug trafficking. Bambi was busted for possession once, and the tabloids dug up her continued dope dealing. I suspect the dope served as another cover. It got Pixy some heavy lifters, in Hans and Franz, and gave the Russians a way to deny involvement, if the deal went south. So, Pixy dealt Bambi in and spotted her a nice chunk of change for hiding the case. She figured with Bambi drawn-in, she could control her even more.

"But when Bambi blew her cut on overdoing her dorm – and her breasts – Pixy got nervous about the attention it would draw. Maybe Bambi also got greedy or needy for another fix and blackmailed Pixy for more. Anyway, when Pixy gave me the slip, it gave her enough time to maybe go to PU to pop Bambi before she could leak the plan."

"Interesting theory about the club, Sonny," Bevel remarked. But this time, it was without the overdose of disregard. It caught me a little off-guard.

Then I realized I might really have been on to something. Like when you're playing cards and you figure out how the guy across from you is bluffing. Bevel figured she was tipping her hand by showing too much emotion. It came across that she was trying to cover-up the truth by trying to dismiss everything I said. And that it didn't bother me made her scramble for another defense.

This time Bevel simply asked me to "continue, please." And she let me finish my deductions in full without trying to throw me off.

"All right," I replied. "Now for Santa Fe: Haji told me it's nearly the Fort Knox of high-tech know-how, meaning not only is it rich in research, but it's well-guarded. Three big military bases in the state could fly tens of jets and send out hundreds of troops in less than an hour to sniff-out and seal-off a sentient steel smuggler's border escape route. In truth, Santa Fe was just a trick that both sides used to try to throw the other off track.

"You said the sting was set up in Santa Fe to catch sentient steel's courier. But you wouldn't have interfered with the courier by taking sentient steel at the Atlas Club, *if* you planned to nab him and his buyer in Santa Fe. Again, Santa Fe was a deception. You lulled Pixy into a false sense of security by thinking your forces were searching Santa Fe.

"And Pixy used Santa Fe to blow Harlan Red-Bull's cover. She chose it as the false meeting place for smuggling Pfannenstiel out. When she confirmed that Red-Bull bought it and relayed it, she switched the pick-up point to City Harbor. When Red-Bull didn't expose the real pick-up point, she knew he was an agent.

"Your man, Harlan Red-Bull, was either an informant or an agent. Either way, he wormed his way into Pixy's posse. Pixy told me Red-Bull threatened Pfannenstiel, meaning Red-Bull gained Pixy's trust and became her enforcer. But in time, Pixy suspected Red-Bull's threats were opportunities to pass information about her plans.

"This is where it gets a little fuzzy, Bev. I'm not sure if you intended for Pfannenstiel to be kidnapped and taken overseas, where he'd be exposed and Pixy likely killed for delivering flawed freight, or if you meant to arrest Pixy and gauge the depth of her involvement. Whatever the case, your fashionable face-to-face with Pfannenstiel at PU panicked Pixy. She realized you were a fed, that she was found out, and that her time was running out. She told the Russians who used their assets to steal your mission code.

"Meanwhile, Pixy hired a patsy – me – to take the fall. She turned everything upside down. You and Red-Bull were out to kidnap Pfannenstiel, not her. You followed us all across town, which gave her time to tie-up loose ends at PU by having Bambi whacked and time to move Pfannenstiel.

"Pixy got to the mansion before you, hid, and kidnapped Pfannenstiel according to plan. Luckily, my bomb-bursting brought the heat—drug enforcement. You used Pixy's drug cover against her, making the arrest look like a bust. And with you and the doc MIA, no one believed me when I told them the bust was really COINTELPRO.

"To sum it up, Bev, this complex caper wasn't about sentient steel or a miracle molecule machine. It was about breaking the mettle of those who would meddle. Bound by budgets, you didn't badger bureaucrats for expensive bullets or brigades to expose the spies. Instead, you used Tinsel Town tactics to cook-up a honey pot of illusions, lies, and half-truths to snare your bear. Charm to disarm: control the criminal from a level he can't comprehend. That's the real revolutionary invention."

Bevel Brand replied, "That's a very, very interesting theory."

After all that, I shouted, *"Theory!* Come on, Bev, you were there. You know damned well that's what happened!"

"I don't know that it happened for *those* reasons," Bevel said softly.

"Cute," I snorted, returning to my senses that I'd lost because I believed a beautiful woman was really paying attention to me. "I should have known you wouldn't buy it. Or more like you couldn't buy it because of your job."

"I believe it would make an interesting scenario for a training exercise."

"Well now, that's original!" I laughed.

Bevel sighed, "Wouldn't it have been so demoralizing to hear me simply say 'I believe you believe it'?"

"Demoralizing would have been you pulling a piece from your coat after I'd finished and saying 'yep, you're right,' and then putting a hole in my head," I answered. "Better yet, doing me in as I walked through the door without letting me spout my deductions."

"Jesus, Sonny, you watch too many f-ing movies!"

"It's either that or selling secrets, if I'm to add meaning to my loser life, right?"

Bevel seemed to recognize a reason she earlier gave for espionage. She swallowed her words with a nodding grin and asked, "There's just one thing I'd like to know, Sonny. If you really believed that sentient steel was more style than substance, why did you let yourself be sucked in?"

I replied, "What guy doesn't like *being sucked in* now and then?"

Bevel wagged her finger at the obvious undertone and said, *"Naughty, naughty."*

I grinned. "Damned woman's intuition," I cursed. "Okay, okay," I gave in. "Why did I fall for it?" I stretched, stood, and plodded to the living room window.

CHAPTER TWENTY-THREE

Blown Away

I flipped up one of the Venetian blinds and watched daybreak bob in and out of the misty morning like a searchlight. "Maybe if I were back home, instead of here, things would have been clearer. I would have seen it all coming a mile away and stayed on the straight and narrow. But that's hard to do here: where the only straight and narrow streets are the back alleys of a barrio or ghetto. The other twist and turn into freeways."

"Freeways with a lot of lanes and few turnoffs," Bevel added softly, knowingly. "I still don't completely know my way around this town."

I managed a laugh. "I don't think anyone ever does, Bev," I said.

"In the intelligence biz, it seems like that everywhere, Sonny," Bevel sighed.

"Yeah, the world's full of freeways nowadays. Most of them lead to some big city – from Beantown to Frisco and every cowtown and tortilla flat in between. But when you get there, you find most cities are full of smog: from all those cars racing to get there, and then wheeling and dealing to stay.

"There was this old guy back home who warned me about this town. He said, "Boy, don't go chasin' pie in that big city's skies." But on TV, it never looks polluted here. They only show endless sunshine and how it brings out the best in people – instant success. I wanted some of that success, so I hoped on an interstate and got outta Dodge. When I got here, I got a new name, a new line of work, and, I thought, a new outlook on life.

"But now, I'm old like that fella back home was. And I see what he was saying. The smog has dulled my senses. That pie I'm forever chasing – my dreams, I mean – always ends up being a cow pie because almost everyone here is full of shit. It's hard telling anymore who's who and what's what. All those freeways, with their fast cars and faster-talking drivers blowing smoke, are the perfect set-up for a set-up."

The scent of perfume drifted into my space by the window. Bevel had joined me. She was already tall, but her sling-back heels lifted her to my height. Bevel looped her arms around my waist and placed her head on my shoulder.

"I'll let you in on something," Bevel whispered

in my ear. "You were right...*about being a patsy, I mean.* We tried warning you of the danger you were in. The taxi chase; taking the empty case from you; Red-Bull's attempts to catch you; and my stabs at trying to talk some sense to you in Golden View Heights – they all failed. So, we assumed you were working for neither side. That you were just a greedy free agent who got tangled up in something he didn't know everything about."

I turned around and asked, "Why didn't you just tell me everything about it in a phone call?"

Bevel made the hand sign for a phone, with her pinky outstretched and her thumb in the air. She raised it to her ear and made a funny face. "*'We're sorry, but you've reached a number that is disconnected or no longer in service,'* Bevel impersonated the smarmy sound of the automated disconnected number message. "Sound familiar, Sonny?"

"*Oh,*" was my weak response. Meiko McCall was right: I needed a cell phone.

I let Bevel continue to promote my patsy status. "When your car was stolen, you tracked it down," she said. "What's one car? Why risk the operation, and your skin, by recovering it? Then, you threatened to kill me and bribe me for sentient steel! Don't worry, Sonny: you can stay employed, supplying us with real criminals to convict."

"*Us?*" I mulled over the word and its meaning

for a moment. "So, am I deputized now?" I asked Bevel.

"Your method of saving the operation by exploding the trunk was brilliant thinking. It taught me not to rely so much on high-tech, but to use my surroundings for solutions. You also taught me to dress down, if I'm going to dish dirt. And your deductions, if nothing else, are well-thought out. My people may have a place for you – a need for someone like you – Sonny."

I laughed, "I'd qualify for the unconscious, white-haired, lab coat–wearing scientist role. And my wonder widgets would be a lit cigarette and a turned-on oxygen tank. Some would call what I did a senior moment, not a method. I was lucky I didn't kill us all! And months of underemployment as a rental cop gave me time to come up with my conclusions about the case.

"But my biggest worry about joining up is the whole counterintelligence setup. I remember the TV show *Mission: Impossible*. The guy on the tape recording always said something like if you're caught, the government will deny your actions. All that hard work for nothing: so you can be tortured, imprisoned, or killed by the enemy? We got each other's back in the steel deal, but would it work out like that in another deal, Bev?

"Thanks for trying to recruit me, but I'm too old and too jaded."

Bevel took exception to the psychoanalysis. "Now that's disinformation if ever I heard it!" she objected. "It's all based on TV series and movies, at that! And so you're 55? They say that fifty's the new…"

My groan got the message to Bevel that I didn't want to be patronized; so she didn't try. And things became quiet for a minute. Bevel sighed and stepped away, leaving me alone at the window.

Then I heard her say, "Well, Sonny, maybe this tidbit of information will cheer you up. Recruitment was only part of the reason I came by."

That aroused my interest. *"Oh?"* I replied, my eyes returning inside from looking out the window.

From a distance, Bevel locked a steady stare on me. She began to sashay and play with the sash that bound her black raincoat. The song she danced to was audible only to her. She probably thought it was a secret that Sonny couldn't crack. But I already knew the type of tune because of Bevel's dance steps.

Marvin Gaye, Barry White, or Teddy Pendergrass – or their modern-day makeovers – were probably grooving and getting Bevel to twist and turn in the tantalizing way women do when they have men locked in dimly lit, smoky rooms. And their only design is to turn men on to turning their pockets out for dollar donations.

Unhurriedly, Bevel undid the sash and then whisked it from its loops and tossed it over her shoulder. Finally, the female fed went for the last line of defense: the raincoat's row of buttons. She popped one loose, then two, and three. Finally, the fourth button came free, and with it, the raincoat. Bevel rolled her shoulders and the coat slid down and pooled at her feet, leaving behind what was a bare, toned torso and long, lithe legs.

The sun picked the perfect time to shine. It finally broke through the chrome cloud cover and beamed through the Venetian blinds like a spotlight, revealing the unbelievable light brown beauty that was Bevel Brand's body. A few bruises and nicks here and there – naturally. But overall, Bev was mind-boggling...*for a fed.*

She revealed something else to me, too. "I saw that in a movie once and always hoped to do it for the right guy," she added. "Thanks, Sonny, for bailing me – I mean, our country – out."

"D-don't mention it," was all I could sputter, still unsure if what I was seeing was real or more smoke and mirrors.

Bevel moved closer to me. Her caress across my stubbly cheek let me know it was real – that she was for real. Bevel then asked, "What do you mean, 'don't mention it'? You collared three bad guys and saved the day. But you didn't get the girl. Well, here I am, Sonny. My body's the bomb. And if you want it, I hope you remember how to 'duck-and-cover' because every minute we'll spend will be a blast!"

I grinned. "Nah," I said. "No more ducking and

covering, Bev. I think I just want to finally stand up and be blown away."

The female fed got in my face, touched my shoulders, and then moved her hands slowly, delicately down my arms. She lowered to her knees, hiked an eyebrow, and grinned like the devil. *"I think that can be arranged, baby,"* she said.

I was being sucked into another situation, but this time didn't mind. Nor did it seem to trouble my gracious government guest.

CHAPTER TWENTY-FOUR

Ticket Out

Fighting crimes and creating crimes to fight kept Bevel Brand busy. So it didn't surprise me when she said that she hadn't been to the beach.

"Let's steal a little time, instead of steel, and go," I suggested. Bevel agreed and left my apartment to change.

With my utilities shut off, I had to engineer a bath. So, I dumped the mix of melting ice and water from my improvised beer cooler fridge into my tub. I sloshed the ice until it melted and waited about fifteen minutes for the whole thing to warm some. Then, I climbed in, splashed about in what amounted to a large puddle, lathered, splashed clean, and dried myself off. Next, I asked my next door neighbor for a hot cup of water. I dumped it into my bathroom sink and shaved.

Once finished, I changed into a cream-colored, long-sleeved polo shirt, khakis, and a worn pair of tan canvas deck shoes: all standard beachwear for this time of year when the beach can look beautiful, but still turn out to be a blustery, bitter bitch.

When Bevel reappeared at my place around noon that Saturday, she sported a zip-up hoodie that was the color of rosé and felt like velour. And except for a pony tail, her beautiful hair was buried beneath a ball cap that had the bold, white inscription "You Don't Know Me" printed across it. Bevel told me it referred to the Witness Protection Program – a souvenir she picked up at a D.C. WPP conference.

Bevel wasn't in the program, but the label fit because I almost didn't know her (after the raincoat consolation prize she'd provided me earlier). And while Birkenstocks replaced her sling-backs, I cheered up once I looked up because Bevel's bare legs were still in plentiful supply. They boldly overflowed her cut-off blue jean shorts.

We left the apartment only to realize I'd forgotten my car keys. Bevel stopped me from going back inside. "Want to ride in movie star style?" she asked.

"What do you have in mind?" I asked curiously, cautiously.

Bevel's only response was to wave a follow-me finger. So I locked up and tagged along. Outside, parked across the street, was a brand spanking new, baby-blue-colored Ferrari. I turned to Bevel in disbelief. *"Yours?"* I asked.

"Ours: it's federal property," she replied. "It's a loan for my next assignment."

"Tired of tailing suspects by taxi, huh?" I teased.

Bevel's rental coupe came complete with all leather, sparkly alloy-trimmed interior and was tricked out with top-of-the-line stereo, climate control, and 620 horsepower to propel it. Bevel asked me (with a straight face) if I wanted to drive it.

I gasped, "Are you kidding! How much does this thing cost, $50,000?"

Bevel shrugged. "About $100,000, give or take the options," she estimated.

"What happened to using your surroundings, instead of high tech, for solutions?"

"I did. When you're in a city full of stars, you need to shine too, right?"

"You got me, there," I laughed.

"Besides, most of the people here are crazy about their cars."

I let Bevel take the helm, while I prepared to navigate. But Bevel spoiled that when she told me the Ferrari was equipped with that computerized car chart system that leads you to your destination. *What didn't this car have?* Then it hit me: atmosphere.

I went back inside and got my CD case. I popped one of my favorite Lisa Stansfield CDs into the Ferrari player. Bev revved up and we raced away, cruising in cool comfort for the scenic shorelines south of town to the smooth, lounge sound of "In All the Right Places."

It was about 2:30 PM when we arrived at Seaboard South. We parked and made our way down to the boardwalk where we picked up some ice cream – Bevel's treat. It was peach for me; pistachio for Bev. Then we lost the crowds of beach blanket bums and bunnies, bawling brats, and the volleyball benders and finally found the secluded stretches of shoreline.

Bevel and I strolled barefoot along the breezy ocean's edge, watching the waves rise and fall with ease, until the sun began to set. I walked up a slope leading from the shore to a spot of dry sand. I took a seat, dug my toes in, and waited for Bevel. She busily collected pebbles below. Once she had enough, she saw me wave and sauntered up the slope.

"What's with the rocks?" I asked Bevel: "Souvenirs?"

"*Protection*," the female fed deadpanned. "I left my gun and badge, remember?"

Bevel developed quite a sense of humor; I laughed hard. But it soon settled. And so did my eyes; on the distant, orange-and-blue-bathed horizon. I realized I was too quiet for too long because Bevel elbowed me. She offered, "A nickel for your notions, Sonny."

"Bev, the days of the private detective are almost done," I mourned. "Open marriages are closing down divorce cases. Open borders mean open trade and cheaper goods. So if your stuff's stolen, don't waste paying my fee of $200 a day plus expenses to track it down. Just buy lower-priced knock-offs at some big bargain barn. And anybody with the internet can do my job: that is to track down names, numbers, and make contacts. Nowadays, life's an open door, if you have the key."

Bevel told me to quit feeling sorry for myself. "The market changes," she said. "And the key to getting ahead is to adjust, Sonny."

I grunted, "That's easy for you to say. You're what, twenty-five or twenty-six?"

"I'm just saying that a lot of that free information you complain about is excess. And some is just bogus. Someone will always pay for verification. You could even go back to school and take some computer classes; a lot of companies hire computer geeks as investigators to dig up data on competitors, or to protect their stuff from being stolen. If you want to get ahead, you gotta get with it, *comprendes*?"

"Stop being your grandfather's gumshoe, huh?" I groaned.

"Something like that, Sonny."

Bevel was wise beyond her years, and put me at ease. "If I can get used to a field-of-12 NCAA football play-off system; the Rams moving back to town; and the Jacksonville Jaguars leaving for London, I guess I can bend with the breeze some more."

"Why do men have to compare everything to sports?" Bevel asked.

"What can I say but life's a ball," I joked. "At least it has been with you, Bev."

Bevel's eyes rolled. But a guilty little grin gave away that she was flattered. Then she shuddered and drew her legs close to the velour warmth of her hoodie. "You should have dropped a dime on the temperature dip, Sonny," Bevel said.

I frowned. "I don't have a dime," I sighed. "Anyway, you're in the intelligence biz: you should've known. Besides, I didn't want you taking another month or more to return. By then, it would be bikini season, and you'd have to leave and change again!"

"I think it's more like you didn't want me to change... *period.*"

I smiled. "How well you know me. Is it that damned female intuition, again?"

Bev mocked my past words. *"I'm in the intelligence biz!"* she said. "Well, today was cool for me too–never mind the sea breeze. I even dig your taste in tunes: *Lisa Stansfield, right*?"

"She's a white Brit, but doesn't sound like it."

"Speaking of 'not sounding like it,' there's something you never made clear, Sonny. Why did you change your name from Rinaldo Weathers?"

"It was a break from the past," I said. "I hated being called Rinty: you know, like the German shepherd?" When Bevel shook her head no, I had some explaining to do. "*Rin Tin Tin* was a Saturday morning show when I was a kid. The dog was the hero; and "Yo Rinty" his call to action. Rinaldo starts with R-i-n, so the kids tagged me with it. As for Weathers, I thought there wasn't any out here, other than sunny. So I dropped it, and took on *Sonny*, instead.

"I figured I'd take advantage of the large Hispanic population here, and went with the last name "Busco." It means "I look for" in Spanish. Clever handle for a P.I., huh? Until I realized I couldn't speak a lick of Spanish to the Hispanics who called me."

Bevel laughed, "That's the most imaginative name change story I've heard!"

"Thanks," I said. "When I asked Quo whether you got me off the hook, he said my story about you was Oscar-caliber…"

Suddenly, what Quo said got me thinking. Oscars are awarded to movies. Then it hit me – or more like punched (as in a ticket – *my ticket out*). "Bev," I began, "they say every cloud has a silver lining. Out here, that silver lining is a cable that plugs into a silver screen. Our adventure could be shown to everyone willing to pay $15 a ticket!"

Bevel Brand tried to return to fed form. She asked, in a silky-sinister way, "What do you have in mind, Mr. Busco?"

Then, I lost my head. "A movie: a big screen

blockbuster about my biggest case!" I burst with glee. "It would all be fictionalized, of course."

"*Mister Busco!*" Bevel snapped.

I calmed down. "You're right," I said, "maybe I should think made-for-TV first – like *Dragnet*. We could show a disclaimer, if you're worried about protecting…"

"I'm worried about protecting you, Sonny! Forget the whole idea!" Bevel warned me. I felt those rocks she collected were being readied to pelt me for my big picture plans. And Bevel's strict school-teacher tone brought me crashing back down from the clouds. I sat on the sand, sulking again.

Then there was a sigh, but not mine. It came from beside me. "Oh, what the hell," Bevel surrendered to me: "At least you're trying. I've even got the perfect title for you movie: *Sonny Busco's Goose Chase.*"

"*Starring Bevel Brand?*" I prodded. "Face it: you have West Coast wiles." When Bevel laughed, I tried to sweeten the deal. "Okay, okay: what if I changed the title to *Venus Spy Trap*, and make *you* the star?"

"*Venus Spy Trap?*" Bevel remarked. "Sounds like a porno, Sonny."

"Now what would an upstanding federal agent know about such things?"

"I wasn't *always* a fed, Sonny."

"And you won't *always* be one," I said.

"That time would come very soon, if I was seen

worldwide in a movie!" Bevel laughed. "Thanks, Sonny, but for the good of the country, I'll pass on being an actress."

Her mind was made up, so I gave up. "You're still destined for stardom, Bev," I still had to add, "but not here. With all your sand, you'll end up on top of the heap. Probably as the director of that alphabet soup snoop group of yours, someday."

Bevel's nose scrunched into that what-the-hell wrinkle. *"Sand?"* she asked. "As in my hair, between my toes, and…?"

Just great! I groaned to myself. With all my back-in-the-day sayings, I'd managed to widen our already considerable age gap to Pacific Ocean proportion.

"Uh, sand…," I began explaining the meaning: "It's an old cowboy phrase. It means willpower, guts, drive, and character. I think your generation calls it *skills*, right?"

Bevel's face warmed into an accepting smile, and she squeezed my arm tenderly. "Thanks, Sonny," she said softly. "To a gal like me – who never thought she'd get out from behind her D.C. desk – that means a lot."

"And I hope I get a lot from *Goose Chase*," I said. "Thanks for the green light and for everything else. The sympathy sex, the stroll, and maybe, above all else, your suggestions: they're all impossible to remove from my mind. You've really got a lot of sand, Bevel Brand."

"Well not in my hand," she replied. The rocks Bevel clutched for protection finally spilled from her hand back onto the sand. "You've disarmed me, Sonny."

"Wait a minute, Bev! Surely you know the L.A. Basin's as nasty as the Roman Colosseum was. Full of robbers, killers, and even bears!"

"*Oh, my,*" Bevel sighed, her voice implying reawakened passion, not panic.

Bevel caressed my cheek, and I gently touched the brim of her ball cap. Pinching together my fore-finger and thumb, I reached over and lifted the cap off her head. Bevel undid her pony tail and shook her head. Her good-looking locks finally fell free.

Our heads swirled sideways. Then our eyes shut and lust led our lips into a locking position that let up only to allow our tongues to plunge and roll around each other's mouths like roller coaster cars. And all of it gave me the childhood ride's same soaring excitement, from my head down to my toes.

After a while we stopped kissing and I placed my arm around Bevel. She snuggled close, and we just sat, silently watching the waves grow larger, the wind louder, and the sun smaller and softer.

Bevel asked me, "What are you thinking, Sonny?"

"About that kiss, of course," I replied "As strange as it sounds, all that French tongue-tangling gave me another idea."

Bevel sighed, "Is that all it meant to you: *an idea*?"

"Well, no. It meant passion, perfect pleasure…, and two other words that start with "P": Pistachio and peach."

"You forgot one more "P" word, Sonny."

"*P.I.?*"

"No. *Promotion*: I feel one coming on," Bevel groaned.

"Hear me out, Bev. For a split second – only a second – it popped into my mind that the ice cream we had could make for an exciting new flavor: passionate pistachio-peach. Do you think I could market that?"

Bevel turned. She smiled at me and said, "Only if *Goose Chase* lays an egg."

"*Precisely,*" I replied.

Bevel turned to me and said, "Not precisely. *Promise*, Sonny."

I looked at her and was a little misty-eyed when I replied, "Promise: something I haven't had in a long time…until now. Absolutely…*promise*, Bev."

The vast Pacific's strong surge swelled. Wave after pounding wave threatened to soon reach even the slope where we sat safely so far. The sands did run out. The ocean poured in, and the tears poured out. It was over.

CHAPTER TWENTY-FIVE

In a Lesser Light

I never saw Bevel Brand again after we left the beach. That wasn't a surprise nor was it particularly painful...*after a while*. We both knew it wasn't going anywhere – that it couldn't go anywhere (given our ages, attitudes, and lifestyles).

Still, I dreamed constantly about her the first month after the beach. Unshakable illusions took hold and convinced me we could make it all work. But the nature of my job – rooting out the truth – forever fouled up the fantasies.

Bevel would vanish into the field for too long, hunting down wayward eagles and prowling bears. And with her implied Witness Protection connections, good luck finding her! But what if I did find her one day? Only crippled physically or mentally by someone better, faster, stronger than her. Did

I – now 56 years old – have the power to help her overcome her wounds or maybe to redirect her life, her training for another life's work?

I decided that at my age, I didn't have the energy or time to keep digging to find the real Bevel Brand. What I'd found was she was notches above the typical fed and was the wish of every woman: to be brilliant, beautiful, and meaningful.

But sadly, Bevel's brilliance and beauty weren't meant for winning the dating game. Instead, they were for hunting game: for sizing up the opposition through binoculars, for the catch, and through gun sights, for the kill. I told myself Bevel could never love anyone as much as she did her country. That she would connive and kill for it alone.

Bevel was definitely brilliant and meaningful. For the steel deal being her first time in the field, she showed some surprisingly sly spy-catching skills and could hold her own in any exchange – verbal or physical. With a little more practice, she'd be a goddess of a G-Woman.

Clearly, Bevel was beautiful beyond doubt. But she strived to turn it into a practical, instead of pedestal, kind of prettiness. With her mysterious complexion – a skin tone whose source I still can't solve – she could be stirred into many situations safely. And the way Bevel brandished her other girly guiles was like a surgeon's scalpel: her razor-sharp chic quickly sliced into, then stripped away, and finally cut out the enemy's memory. Suddenly, instead of the secrets it sought, the other side has eyes only for Bevel Brand. And in the end, they're caught with their pants down – busted. It was easy to see why they planted her in the field.

In the end, I settled on selling myself that my time with Bevel Brand was like the times with the professional strippers, escorts, and other female entertainers I'd hired to test many men's marital devotion.

Big bucks and small talk get these women out of their stuffed, stretched blouses and flimsy skirts and into your bed. But even when they're totally naked—when you think you're seeing all there is to see—you feel there's something they're holding back. That what you're getting is faked or hyped.

What they're hiding is their soul: an impenetrable fortress of deeply layered feelings, faults, desires, and dreams that remains closely guarded. The floozie front fogs most men's view so that no amount of money will *truly* let you see everything. Only what women decide is "the right guy" has a shot at experiencing everything they keep secret.

And though it would rub many women the wrong way to be compared to an adult entertainer – high class or ho – I suspected Bevel most likely wished I thought of her in that lesser light, in order to protect her cover from slipping into sentimentality's snare. Like Delilah, Bevel was soft and sensual on the outside – a player. But on the inside, she was stronger than Samson: a stone-cold slayer at heart, but one able to keep it secret.

I enjoyed my time with Bevel for what it was worth: payment for my steel deal deeds. And now, it was done. But I wasn't.

My next search was through Los Angeles and its surrounding hills – specifically the Hollywood Hills – to shop *Goose Chase*. With the help of an agent – a kind different from Bevel Brand, I mean.

Epilogue

As for *Goose Chase*, the idea proved to be a nest egg after all. A motion picture company (that was a step down from tinsel town's top dogs) bought the rights to my *made-up* misadventure. They even retained me as a "technical advisor." It was obvious that *Goose Chase* would never be Oscar caliber. So, instead of waiting to thank all the little people who made me great on stage, I made sure to spread my good fortune early.

Keeping my promise to cut Salvador Khan in on the deal for loaning me a gun, the company planned to use some of his merchandise in the picture. Sal was kind of a props guy, I guess. He didn't care about that, just that Estado Dorado's Wheel and Deal got more publicity.

Then, for loaning me the Stealth, I fit Hub

Wheeler into the picture. What producer wouldn't have a field day searching his used car lot for stunt cars? I also figured the lovely Meiko McCall might even catch a break in a walk-on role. And the Skyview Lounge is a Hollywood dream set on its own, with the bar's great view, colorful interior, and Joey DiFatino's behind-the-bar banter.

I even looked up zany Zen Prattle: the lady with the SUV who'd saved me from Harlan Red-Bull. I didn't call her personally, but gave the studio her number, instead. If they could fit Zen in, she'd make for good comic relief.

Despite all my good intentions, *Goose Chase* is currently in what they call "production hell." That is, the company's squabbling over directors, writers, and casting concerns. Most of it is probably my own fault, for getting together such a contrasting group of friends to help produce the picture! I once thought the production hold-up was some more of Bevel's creative cooking: to keep *Goose Chase* from being made at all.

But frankly, I no longer care if *Goose Chase* ever becomes a movie. My agent tells me my near–six-figure option deal and technical advisor retainer is rare. He said it's normally lower for those breaking into the business. And that it gets higher the more times you option your script.

Oddly enough, some of what I thought was techno-ethics club twaddle actually turned out to help me financially. Haji Savante said, "don't re-invent the wheel; just add better rubber." So, instead of going hog-wild and buying new stuff with my *Goose Chase* gold egg, I kept my old digs; traded in the Olds for a used car with 50,000 miles on it; and got a cheap cell phone that you feed money into (but only when *you* want to).

However, I decided to quit Coast is Clear and to semi-retire from detecting. I still occasionally take on a case for lawyers who need legwork done, or work on-the-house for a client who really needs the help. And, of course, I can't pry myself away from an occasional marriage infidelity case. Instead of a cheap chore, they provide cheap thrills (and an easy date or two).

Yep. I finally have a life of simple pleasures and financial stability – stability that I still have to guard against getting careless with. But the most comfort in life comes from the simple knowledge I learned while working the convoluted steel deal. The truth about life is that it ain't so simple because the opportunity everyone's after often knocks at odd hours. And, it seems it's when your guard's down, you don't have your A-game going, and you're in your underwear—a holey pair, at that.